THE PRINCIPLE

Jérôme Ferrari

THE PRINCIPLE

Translated from the French
by Howard Curtis

Europa Editions
214 West 29th Street
New York, N.Y. 10001
www.europaeditions.com
info@europaeditions.com

This book is a work of fiction. Any references to historical events, real people, or real locales are used fictitiously.

First Publication 2017 by Europa Editions

Translation by Howard Curtis
Original title: *Le principe*

Library of Congress Cataloging in Publication Data is available
ISBN 978-1-60945-352-7

Ferrari, Jérôme
The Principle

Book design by Emanuele Ragnisco
www.mekkanografici.com

Cover photo: courtesy of Werner Heisenberg's heirs

Prepress by Grafica Punto Print – Rome

Printed in the USA

CONTENTS

The master whose oracle is at Delphi neither speaks
nor hides his meaning—but gives a sign.
—HERACLITUS, *fragment 93*

And He said to me: Between words and silence,
there is an isthmus where the grave of reason
and the graves of things are found.
—AL-NIFFARI, *The Stayings*

POSITIONS

Position 1: Heligoland

You were twenty-three years old, and it was there, on that desolate island where no flower grows, that you were first granted the opportunity to look over God's shoulder. There was no miracle, of course, or even, to be honest, anything remotely resembling God's shoulder, but to give an account of what happened that night, our only choice, as you know better than anyone, is between metaphor and silence. For you, there was first silence, then the blinding light of an exhilaration more precious than happiness.

You couldn't sleep.

You waited, sitting there at the top of a rocky outcrop, for the sun to rise over the North Sea.

And that's how I imagine you today, your heart pounding in the night on the island of Heligoland, so alive that I could almost join you there, you whose name, lost in the grayness of an endless bibliography among so many other German names, was at first, as far as I was concerned, only that of a strange, incomprehensible principle.

For three years, in Munich, Copenhagen, and Göttingen, you'd been wrestling with problems so fearsomely complicated that even the innocent, optimistic young man you were then had sometimes, like his comrades in misfortune, to curse the day when he'd had the preposterous idea of meddling in atomic physics. Your experiments kept yielding ever more results that were not only incompatible with the most established tenets of classical physics but scandalously contradictory, results that were absurd and yet irrefutable, making it impossible to form as much as a slightly sensible image of what was happening inside an atom, or even any image at all. But on the island of Heligoland, where you'd come, your face disfigured by allergies, to protect yourself from pollen, and perhaps from despair, you discovered that the blessed time of images was gone forever, just as the time of childhood must always be: you looked over God's shoulder and saw, through the thin material surface of things, the place where their materiality dissolves. In that secret place, which isn't even a place, contradictions are abolished, along with images and their familiar flesh; no vestige remains there that the language of men can describe, no distant reflection, but only the pale form of mathematics, silent and formidable, the purity of symmetries, the abstract splendor of the eternal matrix, all that inconceivable beauty that had always been there, waiting to reveal itself to you.

Without your faith in beauty, you might never have found the strength to lead your mind, as you'd been leading it without respite for three years, to the extreme limits where the exercise of thought becomes physically painful, and your faith was so profound that neither the war, nor the humiliation of defeat, nor the blood-soaked convulsions of abortive revolutions had been able to shake it. The first time you saw your father in uniform, when you were twelve years old, the metal spike on his helmet must have reminded you of the terrifying plumes of Achaean heroes, and when, just before leaving, he bent to kiss his two boys, your brother Erwin and you, Werner, didn't you quiver at the epic breath of History that had transformed Professor August Heisenberg, before your very eyes, into a warrior? In the station, the farewells, the songs, the tears, and the flowers expressed something higher than a rough or innocent joy, the certainty of sharing a common destiny, which demanded of every man that he take the risk of sacrificing his life to it, because it was from that destiny that any individual life drew its value and its meaning, the thrilling sense of being nothing now but the physical part of a magnificent spiritual whole, and as you watched your father and your two cousins leave, you may have regretted the fact that you were too young to go with them. But the first of your cousins died, and when the second one came back on leave, you didn't recognize him.

Did you guess then what it costs sometimes to look over God's shoulder?

For God, whatever that metaphor designates, is also the master of horror, and there is an exhilaration in horror, more powerful perhaps than the exhilaration of beauty. It's the exhilaration that seizes men when they're surrounded by severed limbs, the stench of corpses fusing with the earth, clusters of worms oozing from wounds like living dough, the red eyes of rats nestling in the darkness of open chests, but even more when they realize the depth of the abysses they've unwittingly harbored inside themselves.

We reach out our hand to our rifle in the darkness of the trenches and we recognize it as an archaic gesture, infinitely older than History, a savage, primordial gesture whose essence hasn't been altered by the shells, the gas attacks, the tanks, the planes, and all the monstrous efforts of modernity, because nothing will ever alter it.

We run until we're breathless, we fall headfirst and watch our own blood gush out, we watch anxiously for white traces of brain matter to appear, but there's only blood, and Lieutenant Jünger gets up again and continues running, his heart overflowing with the intoxication of a hunter, waiting for the ecstasy of that moment when the face of the enemy will rise up from the earth in all its nakedness, when the struggle will finally commence, the loving, mortal struggle so long desired, from which we shall not get up again.

The exhilaration of horror sometimes resembles that of beauty. We're part of a whole that's much greater than we might imagine, greater than the mediocrity of our dreams of comfort and peace, greater than the warring nations, so disproportionately great that the grip in which it holds men can only be maintained by breaking them. The excitement, the intoxication subsides all at once, the veil is torn asunder, and all that is left is to keep running, screaming in terror like an animal, fleeing the ugliness of death, fleeing also what we've become, searching for a refuge that exists nowhere, and Lieutenant Jünger is shaking all over by the time he gets back to the German trenches; tears in his eyes, he writes in his notebook: when, oh, when will this damned war be over?

Perhaps you vaguely glimpsed in the dazed expression that made your cousin unrecognizable when he came back from the front the existence of things it's best not to know about. Horror too may become an object of irresistible desire, as those who had experienced its exhilaration had learned, Lieutenant Jünger and your cousin, perhaps your father, even though he never talked about it—but you, how do you learn it?

The war was over.

Life went on painfully, with its anxieties, its countless bereavements, its hopes and resentments, but beauty became visible again and your eyes were able to recognize it, like the goddess, in the infinite diversity of its mortal forms, all of which you loved. Most men aren't so disgustingly lucky, I hope you were occasionally aware of that: they're sensitive only to one or two kinds of beauty, and so blind to all the others that they can't even conceive the possibility of them. For Professor Ferdinand von Lindemann, who'd agreed to see you at the University of Munich, mathematics possessed the exclusive privilege of beauty and whoever envisaged studying it seriously, as you'd shyly told him you did, had to be convinced that this was an eternal, self-evident truth. Hardly surprising, then, that when, in a bold outburst of frankness, you confessed that you were reading a physics book, worse still, one with the terrible title *Space-Time-Matter*, he gave you a disgusted look, as if he'd suddenly discovered the stigmata of a loathsome disease on your body, and told you that you were forever lost to mathematics, while his dog, a nasty little runt hiding under his desk, to which, in the course of their long companionship, he'd mysteriously transmitted his sense of aesthetics, suddenly started barking as additional testimony to the extent of your ignominy. As far as von Lindemann was concerned, physicists, even potential physicists of eighteen, were unworthy of respect, not just because of their notoriously casual and shameful use of mathematics, but above all because they were damaged individuals, so corrupted by their regular contact with the world of the senses that they openly admitted their perverse interest in something as contemptible as matter.

If Professor von Lindemann hadn't reacted so viscerally, and had taken the time to question you, he would have had to admit that he'd been unfair to you because, deep down, you yourself never believed in matter. In your schoolbooks, the depiction of atoms as small, solid round bodies, joined to each other by obliging hooks, had immediately seemed to you a product of either naivety or deception, two unforgivable sins in the realm of knowledge. When Franz Ritter von Epp entered Munich at the head of the Württemberg Freikorps to crush the Bavarian Socialist Republic, you were lying on a roof, in the warm spring air, ignoring the fighting to read Plato, and you'd discovered how the demiurge creates the world by combining a small number of primitive geometrical forms. In spite of the repugnance you first felt for this unfounded assertion, expressed with all the arbitrary authority of a prophetic revelation and full of scorn for the patient work of reason, you'd been unable to forget it, and had ended up recognizing the triangles of the Timaeus, with a kind of dread, as the metaphorical expression of one of your deepest beliefs, which you'd never formulated and which you didn't even realize was so profoundly yours: what makes up the substance of the world is not material.

Did your dread abate or was it, on the contrary, brought to a peak when you understood how familiar this immaterial thing was to you? Wasn't it into its mysterious proximity that the transparency of mathematical forms, music, and poetry, the peaks of the Alps emerging into the sunlight from a chasm of mist, and all the numberless paths of beauty had always led you? It was an immaterial thing, and yet so tangible you couldn't possibly doubt its reality: it had banished the ghosts of war and revived your joy as you listened to Bach's D minor chaconne rise from a solo violin in the courtyard of Prunn Castle; it had lit up the ruins of Pappenheim over which darkness fell for you alone one summer night in 1920; and if you hadn't encountered it before, perhaps you wouldn't have recognized it on Heligoland, even though it was present everywhere, in the austere line of cliffs, in the monotonous swell of the surf, and above all, more dazzling than ever, in the matrices of the new quantum mechanics.

But nothing can be said about that presence, and it cannot be named.

Anyone who refuses to be resigned to silence can only express himself in metaphors.

In Göttingen in 1922, when Niels Bohr revealed to you, with infinite compassion, that your vocation as a physicist was also a poet's vocation, he didn't teach you anything you didn't already know.

But this is the situation: by expressing ourselves through metaphors, we condemn ourselves to imprecision, and, although we might refuse to admit it, there's always the risk of untruth. I wrote that on the island of Heligoland, a place so desolate that no flower grows there, you, Werner Heisenberg, at the age of twenty-three, looked over God's shoulder for the first time. But now I have to correct that.

It wasn't God's shoulder.

And it wasn't the first time.

Position 2:
AWAY FROM HOME, IN A FIELD OF RUINS

I beg you, don't be ashamed. Not you. It wasn't Professor von Lindemann's little dog you were running away from in 1920, but the messenger, somewhat grotesque and repulsive as demonic creatures always are, that fate had chosen to call you sharply to order and put you back on the path that was yours, the path it wasn't up to you to choose even though you risked losing your soul there in a fool's bargain. In Arnold Sommerfeld's theoretical physics seminar, nobody barked angrily at you, nobody looked down on you, nobody tried to humiliate you. You had come home, where for a long time I myself was ashamed to follow you, since it was your fault that I experienced the worst humiliation of my life.

As far as I know, what comes first in the order of things is everything we have to learn. Traditions, laws, a whole history of mistakes and triumphs. The work of beloved masters, the living, the dead, those who want to survive in you, those who accept that you will surpass them. We must take our place in the patient construction of an infinite edifice, the common work of men, living and dead, hoping perhaps to leave, in our turn, something worthy of being learned. We must acquire enough strength to go into battle when fire threatens and we have to rebuild it anew, saving what can be saved.

But you began with the battle, in a field of ruins.

You began with the fire.

In the sphere you had chosen, nothing could be saved. All the attempts at rebuilding led to rickety, unsteady theoretical constructions that seemed straight out of the mystic visions of a madman, and yet it was impossible to cling to a past that had been reduced to ashes. Ever since Max Planck had discovered the universal action quantum, that ill-fated constant *h* that had, in a few years, contaminated the equations of physics with the malign speed of an ineradicable virus, nature seemed gripped by madness: small cracks fissured the old continuity of the flows of energy, light swarmed with strange granular entities, and at the same time, as if that weren't enough, matter began radiating wildly in a ghostlike halo of interferences. Borders that had once been thought inviolable blurred then shattered into pieces. Depending on the experimental framework to which it was subjected, the same phenomenon appeared now like a wave, now like a corpuscle, even though, of course, nothing in the world could be both one and the other, and the more time passed, the more obvious it became that this appalling duality wasn't in any way the exception but the rule, a rule that nobody could understand. All that remained was the depressing certainty that the atom wasn't a miniature solar system within which friendly electrons peacefully pursued their orbit around an easygoing nucleus: the atom transformed all dreams into nightmares, even the most venerable, the dreams of Leucippus and Democritus, the dreams of Anaxagoras and Lord Rutherford, it was a concentrate of nonsense and heresy, a swamp into which reason sank, and yet it was on this swamp that a new home had to be erected, one in which it would again be possible to live.

So the sacred transmission of knowledge, assuming there was still anything to transmit, had ceased to be a priority for Arnold Sommerfeld. In these exceptional circumstances, the students were no longer to be treated merely as novices but considered, if not as colleagues, at least as assistants whose forces, however faltering and indecisive, had to be mobilized to deal with the disaster. And so it was that Arnold Sommerfeld immediately entrusted you with a mass of experimental results, the word of the master of Delphi, who neither speaks nor hides his meaning, gathered in the laboratories by countless Pythias, a silent word, made up of abrupt scintillations, tiny droplets shining through the fog, spectral lines torn from the secret core of things, which it was your mission to explore in order to flush out the mathematical regularities from which the miracle of meaning might emerge—and then that would be the end of all this chaos, but in the meantime, Sommerfeld assured you, without the slightest trace of irony, that it was as enjoyable an exercise as doing crosswords, and to fill the gaps in your knowledge of physics, he would casually refer you to your fellow student Wolfgang Pauli.

No doubt friendship, if this was indeed friendship, is also an enigma. Pauli was extremely brilliant. Modesty not being his primary characteristic, he didn't stoop so low as to pretend he was unaware of his own value or to assume, even out of simple politeness, that others, starting with you, might not be totally devoid of it. He did concede, though, that in those days of ruins and fire, your complete ignorance of physics had to be considered an advantage: at least your mind wouldn't be cluttered with knowledge that had become pointless, which meant that one couldn't in all honesty rule out the tiny possibility that a new idea might germinate miraculously in that uncultivated soil. You sometimes wondered if he was being sincere or simply pulling your leg, because he didn't spare anybody, not even Sommerfeld, whose demeanor he impertinently compared to that of a retired colonel of hussars, and he had no qualms about shocking you with his irreverence. But at night, he would go to bed as late as possible in order to avoid the dreams that would haunt him all his life and that he hadn't yet begun to note down in order to submit them to the wisdom of Dr. Jung. He would wander all night between his desk and alarming dens of iniquity in which you would never set foot, roaming from one alleyway to another until exhaustion brought him back, as it does all of us, to the pitiless dreams from which no loving embrace can ever save us.

In those dreams, made all the more terrible by the gray light of dawn, he never saw his mother, nor the familiar figures from his childhood.

On high blackboards, in a vast deserted amphitheater, he would watch with terror as equations he should have understood and which he knew he would never see again were erased, and however hard he tried to imprint them on his mind, all that remained of them was the vague memory of silent signs sucked back into nothingness, as if a perverse God had yielded him the secrets of his omniscience only for the pleasure of taking them away from him forever.

From the stony mouths of stern masters fell nonsensical maxims he didn't want to hear, in all the languages of the world.

Long golden cobras slithered in the dust, in the shimmering starlight, and he watched the fruit rot on the branches of the tree of knowledge.

Early in the afternoon, he would join you at the University, where you'd arrived early in the morning while he was still moaning in his bed. He would greet you with nonchalant affection, trailing in his wake the odor of alcohol and tobacco and fallen women, all those things that only existed for you in their evanescent form as scents. You were such an utterly wholesome young man, a boy scout eager for fresh air and honest camaraderie, so full of enthusiasm and innocence that you imagined you and your friends in the youth movement were working to bring about a better world, as if hiking, gathering around the campfire in manly and ascetic good humor, and leading a clean and spotless life were enough to redeem the world. You also loved everything that's alien to me, everything I don't understand, and that should have been enough for me to hate you, even though the young man I'm forced to recognize as myself still doesn't know, on this day in June 1989, the extent of the humiliation he will soon suffer because of you, while he's still waiting to be called to take his final end-of-year oral exam.

I've just heard that I'll have to comment on a passage from *Physics and Philosophy*, which of course I haven't read, occupied as I've been in indefinitely prolonging my adolescent crisis, overdosing on English cold wave music and incense. There in front of me is your book, whose cover illustration, so drastically ugly it could only have been premeditated, depicts a horrible orange polygon on a black background, as if the publishers, fearing that quantum mechanics wasn't sufficiently off-putting in itself, had tried to discourage hypothetical buyers by every means possible, even the most underhand—unless they considered ugliness an unquestionable guarantee of scientific seriousness. I hear the candidate before me babble laboriously on, I see his quivering back, his bent neck, and, facing him, the young female assistant professor listening with a slightly tense smile and tapping her fingertips mechanically on the table. I think she's beautiful, and I now regret not having set foot all year in the classes she devoted to you, but I'm not thinking about you, I'm probably being stupid, indulging in vague erotic fantasies, and I'm not scared. I've learned to comment on texts I haven't read and don't understand, when it comes down to it that may even be the one indisputable skill I've acquired after four years of study. A few popular articles, the right methodological jargon, and my own brazen arrogance have so far allowed me to successfully conceal my laziness. So I know that you were responsible for the uncertainty principle, which stipulates, apparently, that it's impossible to determine simultaneously the position and speed of an elementary particle, and I also know that, in the controversy which for a long time divided physicists in the 1920s, for reasons that escape me as totally as they bore me, you, along with Niels Bohr and Wolfgang Pauli, were an opponent of Einstein, Schrödinger, and the Prince de Broglie—and this meager baggage seems to be quite sufficient to confront the young assistant professor, who's now signaling to me to join her. I advance with the unmistakable smugness of ignorance because, basically, I don't know a thing, I don't know you, I don't want to join you on a desolate island, you're still nothing to me but one more German name on an endless list of German names, I know nothing of the joys and sorrows of the life of the mind, I carefully chop up texts into sections and subsections, like cuts of meat, until nothing is left alive, I don't know your unforgettable moments of grace, looking at the North Sea, and I don't know that the unforgettable moments of grace don't solve everything.

No sooner is it glimpsed than the light disappears.

And yet, when you submitted the results of your calculations on Heligoland to Pauli, he didn't greet them as the ravings of a fool, and even deigned to find them "interesting," which, coming from someone who described Einstein's propositions as "not completely stupid," could only be interpreted as a remarkable display of enthusiasm. You were convinced you'd just taken a crucial step on the only road that was still open, the only one leading out of the terrible labyrinth in which you'd all been wandering so sadly for so many years. All you had to do was give up insoluble questions, those that revolved around a physical reality that nobody could observe or conceive, forget all those stories of waves and corpuscles, orbits and trajectories, free yourself painfully from your nostalgia for images, and take one giant leap across the abyss and into the refuge of mathematical forms, because it's there that reason has always had its home—and it was once again the summer night in the courtyard of Prunn Castle, with the notes of the chaconne rising from a solo violin and snatching you from your pain by revealing that the world wasn't just the chaos it seemed to be, that great broken body, with its pointless deaths, its lost souls, its vain hopes, its ruins, its indistinguishable resentment and anger, the humiliation of its diktats, and that it was still possible to have faith in what you didn't call God but a central order, within which everything had its place. Yes, you'd found the right way, the only way, that much was certain, and for a moment, I suppose, you had no doubt that you would convince the community of physicists.

But of course, nothing happened the way you wanted it to.

When you explained the peculiarities of your matrix mechanics to Einstein, he accused you, not entirely unreasonably, of leading physics into a dangerous terrain by abandoning the ideal that had always been his, the objective description of nature. Then, a little later that same year, 1926, Erwin Schrödinger put forward a hypothesis that expressed an unreasonable hope and must have appeared to you a terrible step backwards: that electrons had never been particles but, quite simply, waves, which sometimes looked falsely like particles. In support of his statements, and in order to describe the evolution of these waves of matter, Schrödinger proposed a magnificent differential equation that took account of the experimental results as well as your stern matrices, but in an infinitely simpler and more familiar manner. In doing so, he aroused the enthusiasm of a scientific community delighted, after years of wandering in a quantum storm, to at last see again the shores of the paradise that a jealous God had taken away from it. The professor you admired so much, Arnold Sommerfeld, also seemed ready to succumb to the baleful siren song of these waves, and no matter how strongly you objected that Schrödinger's theory, seductive as it was, contradicted known facts, nobody listened to you, everything would soon be resolved, it was all perfectly obvious, you were even openly suspected of harboring some nasty grudges, you were focusing on unimportant details out of pure jealousy, vexed at having to renounce your quantum ravings. Nobody is free of pretty resentments, and it's quite possible you were indeed suffering from wounded pride, but what motivated you before anything else was the belief that it was necessary to renounce forever the intuitive representations of atomic phenomena, however painful that might be: Schrödinger and all the others were wrong, they were embracing the futile pipe dreams that desire and nostalgia rendered irresistible to them, nothing more, but, without knowing it, they were still wandering in a labyrinth full of monsters, on the borders of a savage land, a hostile land they would have to tame because it wouldn't let them escape, and never again would they find their lost paradise.

Position 3:
IN THE CLOUD CHAMBER

The elements of the problem are simple and depressing: in a Wilson chamber, we can visualize the trajectory of electrons in the form of condensed droplets in the fog; but whatever the theoretical framework chosen, yours or Schrödinger's, it's impossible to suppose that the electrons do indeed follow a trajectory without falling into terrible contradictions.

We are thus seeing something that clearly exists even though it ought not to.

The others were all wrong, you knew that, and Niels Bohr and Wolfgang Pauli knew it too, but the merciless cloud chamber deprived you of the luxury of believing that you'd solved everything and that you were just a poor misunderstood genius. Oh, no, the unforgettable moments of grace don't solve everything, and every advance gives rise to a new disappointment, even crueler than the previous ones. You could only counter an incomplete theory with another theory just as incomplete. You could merely denounce mistakes you didn't have the means to correct by joining Niels Bohr in Copenhagen, where he'd invited Schrödinger in order to impress upon him that, in spite of the considerable mathematical progress represented by his wave function, nothing was settled at the level of physical reality—and in fact he spent days on end trying in vain to make him see that, without giving him a moment's respite. He'd installed him in his own home, in order to make sure that he wouldn't run away, and to torment him as much as he liked: as soon as morning came, he would stand in the doorway of the poor man's room and inform him of the objections he'd come up with during the night; at the breakfast table, he would drive him into a corner with the fierce stubbornness of a fanatic; through the door of the bathroom, he would continue to assert, and implore Schrödinger to accept at last, that the electron, while it might manifest some of the behavior of a wave, could in no way be considered merely as a wave; all day long, he would pursue him from the living room to the study, he would pursue him even into his dreams—so much so that Schrödinger, after regretting bitterly, as seems to have been the rule at the time, that he'd ever made the stupid decision to study physics, had no other way out than to fall ill in order to escape his tormentor. This wasn't much help, because Niels Bohr now laid siege to his sickbed, grabbing him by the lapels of his pajamas and dragging him from his soft slumbers with such inflexible stubbornness that he must have made the prospect of death seem ever more delightful. And when Schrödinger managed to flee his Danish jail, it was you that Bohr now undertook to torment systematically. He would ask you incessant questions, hovering over you like a bird of prey, in a sickening haze of tobacco; he would twist the problems in all directions, grimacing like a man possessed, until they became totally incomprehensible; he would exasperate you, stop you from sleeping, stop you from thinking, until you couldn't bear it anymore and you burst into sobs at three in the morning and begged him to leave you in peace. You welcomed his decision to go on a skiing trip to Norway as an unexpected liberation: it can't be ruled out that you furtively hoped he would break a leg, or even both legs, immediately reproaching yourself for your hardness of heart, because you loved him like a father. But it's necessary to get away from one's father figures in order to be alone and helpless in front of Wilson's cloud chamber, orphaned eyes fixed on a trajectory that shouldn't exist.

It was there that you returned endlessly, it was impossible to escape, the unpalatable taste of reality made you nauseous, and even the thought that, from that point of view, Schrödinger, with his stupid waves, was no more capable than you were of explaining such a simple phenomenon, was no consolation.

But in Bohr's absence, God remembered that he was merciful and let you look over his shoulder once again. And you understood.

In the cloud chamber, the trajectory of an electron could not be observed, and had in truth never been observed. All that could be seen were the particular tracks of drops of condensation, nothing more, and it was the human mind that, victim of a routine that was several thousand years old, connected these tracks into an illusion of a continuous trajectory, just as children carefully join the numbered dots in their drawing books until witches, dragons, and other imaginary figures appear.

You still needed to learn how to look beyond the obvious, to strip yourself of all the habits keeping you captive: somewhere, lost in the cosmic immensity of the droplet, was the electron. It was impossible to say where it was exactly. A little farther on, it again indicated its approximate position but when it came down to it, there was no reason to think that it was the same object leaving traces of its passing in the fog. There was nothing but a sequence of singular events, flashes of fleeting existences lighting up the darkness and then going out again. And that was all. You had seen. There was nothing more to see. No permanence. No continuity. No trajectory—just an army of bloodless ghosts crossing Wilson's chamber at an indeterminate speed, taking vague shape and leaving the imprint of their blurred contours in the mist.

And that's the principle.

But I, decades later, can only repeat: according to Heisenberg's uncertainty principle, in quantum physics it's impossible to determine simultaneously the position and speed of an elementary particle, and I know that things are going very badly, the young assistant professor has stopped smiling completely, the tips of her long fingers hit the table at an accelerated pace in time with her exasperation, the thin lines at the corners of her eyelids plunge me back, at the least appropriate moment, into erotic images from which the terror I'm starting to feel is unable to rescue me. She sighs and slowly passes her hands over her face. I find nothing better to do than to notice that she isn't wearing a wedding ring, at the very moment I know I'm done for, I'd have been certain of that even if her anger didn't tell me that, in all probability, I'm talking complete nonsense, because your publishers have screwed up the production of your book to such an extent that it isn't only hideously ugly but impossible to handle, as I've just experienced; during my short analysis, the binding has snapped and the pages have shamelessly fallen out and spread across the desk, providing irrefutable proof that the work from which they've just dissociated themselves hasn't been opened before today. She gestures for me to be quiet, she's tired of me serving up this stale old dish, a dish I may know perfectly well how to concoct, she's prepared to acknowledge that, because what I'm saying isn't even bad, isn't even false, just the same old tasteless positivist stew she's been served so many times she's sick of it, I'm turning what's actually a terrible verdict of dissolution into a vague precept about the limits of knowledge, and she keeps condemning me, she won't stop until I myself have dissolved into the blinding clarity of a luminous fog. I'd like to be at home, in my room, lying next to the girl who comes to join me after I've sent my mother out for a walk or to do the shopping, making her promise not to come back too early, which she accepts every time, quite happy to remain the backstage organizer of my sex life, with an amused, complicit smile that makes me ashamed, I'm ashamed now, I feel sick to my stomach, I'd like to be far from you again, as I've always been.

I'm so far from you.

I don't know you, I don't know Bavaria, the Alpine peaks in the winter sun, or the castle of the Prince of Denmark on the shore of the gray sea, nature scares me, it disgusts me, and when I listen to the partita for solo violin, I don't hear the call of any central order but merely the strains of an inconsolable sorrow, as if life, with all its profound, pointless strength, were mourning its own fragility. I'm far from your struggles, from your exhaustion, far from the sobs that Niels Bohr, as soon as he returns from Norway, again provokes in the night with his questions, his cruel objections, that sadistic intransigence of his in wanting to understand the principle you've just discovered, refusing to give you any rest until you've fully understood it yourself and formulated it in the language of men.

I'm far from your sleepless nights, from your bursts of hatred, and the sincerity of your remorse when you wrote to Niels Bohr asking him to forgive you for your childish recalcitrance, the weakness of your frayed nerves, and above all your ingratitude, because you love him like a father who, ever since your first encounter in Göttingen, has never stopped teaching you, no, more than that, who's never stopped showing you what thinking is, and, without him, you would never have known that thinking has nothing to do with calculations, logic, or crosswords, but that it's actually a magic spell of speed and power, of cruelty, pain, and ecstasy, the open wound we're determined to make deeper.

I find it hard to understand what thinking means, I find it hard to understand even the language of men beyond which the principle extends, but since it's in the language of men that it must be expressed, let's put it this way: the speed and position of an elementary particle are linked in such a way that any precision in measuring one entails a proportionate and perfectly quantifiable indeterminacy in measuring the other.

If we choose to determine the position exactly, our ignorance of the speed becomes literally infinite—which doesn't mean that this speed exists and we don't know it, but rather that the concept of speed has lost any precise meaning.

If we determine the speed, it's the position that becomes hazy, as if the electron were stretching out in space, filling the whole of it, down to its smallest recesses.

Speed and position are therefore mere virtualities,

which only acquire a modicum of objective reality at the moment of measurement, and never together.

But what the language of men expresses so clumsily can be grasped all at once in an equation of such concision and simplicity as to conceal its poisonous nature. Because well before it took the form of mathematical inequalities, to which it owes its incomparable beauty, the principle first consisted of your belief that we will never get to the core of things, not because of a curse or the weakness of our faculties, but for the radical, conclusive reason the young assistant professor reveals just before she dismisses me, leaning toward me across the table that protects me from her rage and indignation: because things have no core.

Position 4:
BETWEEN THE POSSIBLE AND THE REAL

In bibliographies as in war memorials, names end up turning into lies that conceal what they should designate. They are ageless and faceless, and I hadn't realized how young you were until I saw that photograph taken in 1920, perhaps just as you were joining Sommerfeld's seminar. You're not much more than a child, and it's true, you look like a boy scout, but the innocent smile that lights up your face bears witness to a trust in life so admirable that each time it makes me forget everything that distances me from you. It's a total, spontaneous trust, without arrogance or conceit, which is impossible to ridicule, and it seems as though it's bound to preserve that youthfulness of yours forever, because we find it still intact ten years later, at the University of Leipzig, with only the black armband you're wearing after the death of your father to distinguish you from your students, or in Brussels, in the group photograph of the 1927 Solvay Conference. You aren't in the front row, where Albert Einstein, Marie Curie, and Max Planck are sitting, but, more modestly, standing in the back row, a little stiff and embarrassed, next to Pauli, who seems to be giving Schrödinger a sidelong look. And yet it's your principle that's the focus of all the debates: every morning at the breakfast table, Einstein presents the experiment he's imagined during the night to refute it, an experiment that ought to prove at least the theoretical possibility of determining exactly the speed and position of a particle; and every evening, after a long day of reflection in the course of which he has, as usual, turned the problem this way and that until those around him are completely exhausted, Niels Bohr points out the flaw he's discovered in Einstein's argument and saves the principle until the following morning. But Einstein, supported by Schrödinger and Louis de Broglie, doesn't give up.

He'll never give up.

It has nothing to do with a technical disagreement or a problem of mathematical formalism. Paul Dirac, who's even younger than you, has demonstrated that your matrix mechanics is mathematically equivalent to Schrödinger's wave mechanics, and that they therefore express exactly the same thing, as if they were translations, into two different languages, of a single mysterious text—the word of the master of Delphi, who neither speaks nor hides his meaning, for which mathematics is also a subtle metaphor. You began with the battle, you began with the fire, and now, spending the summer of 1989 in my father's house by the sea, sheltering the bleeding shreds of my self-esteem and trying as best I can to understand what earned me the worst humiliation of my life, I discover that instead of extinguishing that fire, you spread it like a wild man, until it became an immense conflagration, joyously ravaging the Holy of Holies, consuming all the sacred ideals of science in its devouring flames, just as Einstein told you in Berlin in 1926.

You had to have been young, with the youth of conquerors and killers.

You write to your friend Carl Friedrich von Weizsäcker that you've just disproved the law of causality, you can't get over it, and, in the enormity of that statement, entrusted to a fifteen-year-old boy who admires you and dreams of following in your footsteps, there's a mixture of sacrilegious panic, nonchalance, and pride. You're right to be terrified, you've done much more than disprove causality, you've uttered, with the murderous innocence of youth, a verdict of dissolution that transforms the ultimate components of matter into creatures in limbo, paler and more transparent than ghosts—poor things without qualities, so stripped of everything that they become indescribable, barely the promises of things, lost somewhere between the possible and the real, waiting for the gaze of men to turn toward them and call them into existence. For the gaze of physicists is no longer anything but the gaze of men, injecting the venom of subjectivity into everything it touches. It will never be God's gaze. The old man's plans won't be revealed, the most we can hope is to throw a furtive glance over his shoulder, and that's what Einstein can't bear. Neither he, nor Schrödinger, nor de Broglie can agree to give up the unreasonable, magnificent hope that was the raison d'être of their lifelong quest—the hope that one day they would achieve an objective description of the secret core of things—and they can't accept the fact that, thanks to you, that hope should be abolished, unable to survive even as an ideal, because things have no core, the principle places an insurmountable barrier between us and things, an isthmus beyond which stretches an unspeakable void.

It was an honorable battle, a necessary battle, and, even though the future has consistently proved you right, long after all your deaths I sometimes feel like reproaching you for considering from the start, with the nonchalance and naive arrogance of youth, that it was a lost battle—but I don't do so, and I regret thinking that you were nonchalant about it, you weren't, any more than you were naive, in fact you were so far from being naive that it was impossible for you to believe that the whole reality of the world would one day allow itself to be tamed by the familiar concepts of the language of men, you knew that the time would come to yield to the cruel necessity to express, as poets do, what can't be expressed and should be silenced. You knew it, deep down you'd always known it, well before being reminded of it by Niels Bohr on that wonderful day in Göttingen in 1922, when you walk all afternoon beside him for the first time, beneath a limpid spring sky, amazed that he should confide in you like that in spite of your youth and insignificance, as if the recollection of an intimacy much older than your encounter already linked you to him. Listening to him with fervor, you follow him up onto the hills overlooking the city and then well beyond, as far as that place whose existence you've long suspected, which isn't even a place and can only be evoked, as Niels Bohr tries to do with an anxious, feverish, almost sick rigor, in a whirl of metaphors, alternating partial, inexact images without fear of contradiction, for here, he says, the opposite of a profound truth is another profound truth. Here, he also says, nothing can be both clear and precise—and now I understand how much I was misled by the deceptive clarity of your texts, stupidly trusting the simple examples you give only in order to restrict their pertinence and validity. You assert nothing you don't finally question, in a constant movement made up of leaps and retreats and suddenly inverted viewpoints, it's exhausting to follow you in these twists and turns, which contort language every which way with a seriousness all the more respectful and compassionate in that you know you're performing an impossible task—trying to make words say what can't be said but must nevertheless be said. For a long time I suspected you of chronic indecision, naming and renaming the principle with exasperating casualness, as if to add to the confusion, hesitating between *uncertainty*, *indeterminacy*, and that German term, obviously impossible to translate, that means the absence of sharpness, the lack of detail in a poor photograph, where we don't know if the failure is due to a mistake in focusing or because we were trying to capture the fleeting shimmer of an almost nonexistent object, an object without outlines—but I was still wrong; because of their sin, men long ago lost the privilege of looking at the surfaces of things and reading their true names, which remain hidden, and perhaps you found it impossible to choose a single name.

Perhaps you needed all those contradictory names in order for them to come together in some mysterious way and for the true name to emerge from their very discord.

These are difficult things to understand, especially when you've done nothing else but listen to cold wave music and send your overcomplacent mother out shopping as often as possible in order to at last be alone with the girl whose memory stops me from working and distances me from you again, in my father's house in the summer of 1989, because I see her again advancing toward me, inaccessible and naked, as if she came from far away, in spite of the narrowness of my room, I watch her advance, she walks interminably because, thank God, her position isn't clearly determined, and I'm still watching her even as I already huddle in her arms, she walks without seeing me, as if I didn't exist, as if she wasn't coming toward me but going down to bathe naked, on a starry August night, in the coolness of an unknown river, while I watch her, not from a teenager's mattress laid on the floor, but hidden, my heart pounding, behind heavy, scented branches that sway in the breeze, and, when I huddle against her, still watching her walking endlessly, I know that I will never forget this moment when the existence of the mind becomes more tangible, more indisputable, than that of the flesh, in the transparency of the flesh itself. How much closer I should feel to Schrödinger than to you, who burn with an abstract fever; Schrödinger loved women, he loved them so much that on the basis of that indefatigable love he constructed a whole vision of the world, sensing, from having experienced it so often, that flesh too is a vibrating wave.

But what did you know of that, with your unhappy love affairs, your spectral love affairs so long condemned to haunt the misty border between the possible and the real?

You follow Adelheid von Weizsäcker's fragile footsteps as she glides like a ghost through the streets of Berlin and you know that she passed that way, still escaping you, because everything the girl illumined has again become drab and gray. You scared her, her and all her family, starting with your friend Carl Friedrich, with the mystical intransigence of your passion, that abstract fever that consumes and exiles you. You ask too much, your demands are excessive, you'd like every declaration of love to be an epiphany that transforms the world utterly, as it did that night in Pappenheim, and opens a new path toward the invisible beauty of the central order, but nobody understands you.

You write to your mother that destiny is denying you happiness.

Everything escapes you.

All you're left with is the sad pleasure of intangible things, the memory of a hand lightly touched, the promise of a journey that didn't take place, the imperceptible rustle of distant fabrics, the smell of faded flowers, and all the gray streets of so many cities that Adelheid did not illumine with her presence. The abstract fever that is yours spreads, it invades everything. The verdict of dissolution that you uttered falls on your own life. Retired Lieutenant-Colonel Ernst Jünger writes that the atom has lost its substance and become pure form, and that's how the young girl you loved escapes you, not by fleeing but by evaporating before your eyes, becoming ever more diaphanous, and now, while she continues to live far from you and you appear nowhere in her dreams of happiness, all you have left of her is a pale, translucent envelope she unwittingly bequeathed to you, the idea of a girl, an idea nobody will take in his arms, an idea that smiles at you sadly in your immense solitude.

You spoke to your mother about the distant music of essential things, you complained that your life was like a dusty road through an ugly, arid landscape, and without your work your immense solitude would have been absolute. But it wasn't. You had to participate in huge, unending debates, which allowed you to escape both your melancholy and everything that disgusted you in public life, which you didn't take seriously because you found it impossible to believe that the forces of stupidity were infinitely superior to those of reason. If you were naive, it was perhaps in dreaming that, when it came down to it, the world of politics ought to obey the same aristocratic rules as the world of science, in which the fiercest struggles allow no other weapons than arguments and still constitute expressions of friendship and respect. When a cause is defended only by violence, lies, and calumny, you thought, it admits its own weakness, and you were right—but you never imagined the power of weakness, humiliation, resentment, and abject fears. Something subtle and rotten was tainting the air you breathed but you didn't sense it; you conversed fraternally with men of all nationalities who had the same idea as you of what was essential, you went from one country to another, one university to another, in Italy, England, the United States, as if the vast contemporary Athens in which you lived had wiped out borders, you leaped happily onto the corner pillar of a terrace in Japan, and Dirac, terrified at the thought that you might fall at any moment, watched you balance there, your hands nonchalantly plunged into your trouser pockets, impassive and joyful, facing the big clear sky.

That path is neither drab nor gray. It doesn't yet have any of the colors of disenchantment. It leads to Stockholm, where you go in 1933 with Dirac and Schrödinger, who've been jointly awarded the Nobel Prize for Physics; it's also been awarded to you, a year late, for 1932. A year too late. What are you thinking, in your white tie and tails, as the president of the Royal Academy of Sciences begins his solemn speech?

Your Majesty, Your Royal Highness, ladies and gentlemen…

Are you thinking of the sad irony of your resounding success at a time when the girl who doesn't want you to love her has slowly turned into a ghost who may be standing painfully close to you? Or of the SA parading beneath your windows a few months ago, brandishing the torches of victory? Isn't it strange that such a thing becomes real when what should be real remains forever confined to the endless limbo of the possible? It wasn't the wind in the foliage, it wasn't the fog, it was the Erl-King, drunk with a fatal love, the father clasps his child to him, the corpse no heavier in his arms than the memory of a child, no heavier than the absence of Adelheid, the SA parade in triumph and you can't hate them, you can't believe those fine young people will let themselves be deceived by a charlatan for much longer, they'll get over their rapture, but you know nothing of that rapture, you know nothing of power, or the incredible exhilaration of the herd, you can't know that something has just begun for Germany that will only end this month, November 1989, when I sit next to my mother in front of the television and watch incredulously something you would so much have liked to see and won't see, the fall of the wall I thought was eternal and the end of the only world I've known until now. The impossible is becoming real with disarming simplicity. In the city of your birth, while the stone eyes of priests and saints straight out of one of Pauli's nightmares look down impassively, people from the East cross the old bridge over the Main and park outside the Prince-Bishop's Palace in the icy night. On the radio, the mayor asks that they be saved from the danger to which their curiosity and regained freedom have exposed them, that they be taken food and hot drinks and given shelter, and the inhabitants of Würzburg set off to meet those they haven't seen for so long they no longer know them. It's likely they hurt them unwittingly; after a separation of forty years there's something absurd about such goodwill. They stare at their strange clothes and impossible cars; they welcome them with conventional, excessive compassion, not like brothers they thought they would never see again, but like convalescents who have at last recovered from a shameful disease, one with which they were familiar from having suffered it themselves but from which they're proud to have happily recovered much earlier—which is tantamount to telling these other people that their whole lives have been nothing but a long disease.

Professor Heisenberg, it fell to you, while still so young…

There are so many things you can't know, so many things I don't understand, but, if this disease exists, stretching over generations, you must have vaguely felt the first effects contaminating your joy and giving it the bitter flavor of an incurable sadness while the shadow of Adelheid fades away and the President of the Royal Swedish Academy of Sciences salutes you as the founder of quantum mechanics before going on to praise the work of your colleagues.

Professor Dirac.
Professor Schrödinger.

You're alone again, in a place where I can't join you, a place where, in truth, nobody can, waiting to bow to the king who is to give you your prize, and there you are, standing balanced above the void, perched on the pillar of a terrace in Japan, next to Dirac whose anxiety you don't even notice because you aren't looking at him, you aren't looking at anything or anyone, you shyly plunge your hands into your trouser pockets and you're all alone, as if you too are suspended between the possible and the real, against a colorless sky, with your youth still intact, so moving and so pointless.

Speed

Now it's the whole world that you watch fading away on a street corner in Leipzig, one morning in January 1937. You hold out your winter aid bowl to the passersby. In return for their contributions, you give them a badge made out of scrap iron with the arms of Saxony on it, which they pin to the collars of their winter coats before walking on in the cold. You can't remember why you're doing this but it doesn't matter because the world is fading away, the whole world. You look around you, trying to understand what has changed. You can touch the buildings, feel the cold stone beneath your fingers, but you don't trust your sensations.

It's all a lie.

The passersby, the streets of Leipzig, and you yourself are merely characters in a grotesque play intended to rouse the unshakable solidarity of the German people, all of whose members, even eminent Nobel prizewinners, are prepared, as long as the suggestion is insistent enough, to voluntarily sacrifice a valuable part of their time to help the needy by appealing to the unfailing generosity of their compatriots, who spontaneously put their hands in their pockets in a way that warms the heart in spite of the harsh winter weather.

What does it matter that it's all a lie, what does it matter that the whole meticulously planned operation, by making charity and spontaneous generosity obligatory, drains them of their meaning, turning them into an untruth the stench of which upsets you much more than the cold? Truth and lies are now a question of decree and you're no longer allowed to pass a judgement on them.

What does your despair matter?

You're standing on a street corner in Leipzig, you're quite motionless, and yet you're being swept up, at an indeterminate speed, a speed almost nonexistent and almost infinite, in a movement you fear will carry you away forever and which is starting now, just when the whole world is fading before your eyes. You see through the cold stones of the buildings, you see through the bodies of the passersby, not what they conceal, but what they are, ruins as shaky as a stage set, bathed in phosphorus light, a heap of dusty rubble, lying in the shelter of tall, pointless walls, in a terrible chaos of white-hot stones, collapsed floors, melted silverware, and metal beams twisted like broken bones, and amid these ruins hurry corpses who only keep moving through the winter morning because they think they're alive, nobody having yet informed them that they are long dead, and doomed like the whole world to the inescapable punishment of unreality: they're no longer even corpses but simulacra, lost souls refused even the charity of damnation. You should feel mortally sad but you can't, you're nothing but a pure, disembodied gaze contemplating the disaster and you can no longer remember who you are, or even if you were once somebody.

Please let me help you.

Your name is Werner Karl Heisenberg.

You're thirty-five years old and, among other essential things, you're a physicist.

Tonight, you're expected at the house of some friends to play the piano part in a Beethoven trio.

The mirror held up to you by the proximity of your fellow men, those lost souls who persist in a parody of life, seems to you much harder to bear than solitude and you would prefer not to go.

Out of loyalty, weariness, or politeness, you'll go anyway.

There you'll make the acquaintance of Fräulein Elisabeth Schumacher, whose gaze as she watches you playing will remind you, along with the music of Beethoven, that reality can't be entirely abolished, even by decree, any more than can the distinction between lies and truth, which is still preserved somewhere, out of the reach of men. Nothing will ever seem to you as real as that gaze, which you won't even need to return in order to feel your hands come back to life on the keyboard and your heart fill with the trust you thought was lost. You're so tired of dealing with ghosts. It's high time you let them go.

You remember now: your name is Werner Heisenberg, you're thirty-five years old, and this evening you will meet your wife. But for the moment, you're standing on a street corner in Leipzig, and the world that's entirely fading away before your eyes is one, I'm sorry to tell you, that you will never see again.

The movement that sweeps you away may not have received its first impulse in Leipzig in 1937 but, without your being aware of it, so imperceptible was its incredible speed at the time, many years earlier, in 1922, in the very same place —there's no doubt as to the position, which is determined with all the required precision. You'd taken a room in a shabby hotel, the only one you could afford, in order to attend, on the advice of Sommerfeld, who'd paid for the trip, a lecture by Einstein, whom you didn't yet know. I can imagine how happy you were at the thought that the mysteries of the theory of general relativity, about which all you knew was what Wolfgang Pauli had consented to explain, would soon be expounded to you out of the very mouth of its creator, who might agree, provided Sommerfeld introduced you, to answer in detail and in person the countless questions you wanted to ask. Such joy can only go hand in hand with extreme vulnerability, and I also imagine the pain of your disillusion when, on reading the pamphlet a student stuffed into your hands at the entrance to the lecture hall, you abruptly learned two depressing facts: the first, that science was not a inviolable sanctuary, forever preserved from the stains of ideology and politics; and the second, equally regrettable although infinitely less tragic, that winning the Nobel Prize wasn't a lasting guarantee against idiocy. In 1905, the Nobel Prize had indeed been awarded to Philipp Lenard, the author of the pamphlet, in which, without the slightest restraint, he poured out a torrent of abuse against Einstein, whose theory of relativity expressed the quintessence of an appalling, typically Jewish physics, which everywhere bore the pernicious marks of a typically Jewish hostility to common sense, as well as a typically Jewish taste for unfounded theoretical speculations, sterile paradoxes, and the use of sufficiently obscure mathematics as to lead innocent, good-natured Aryans astray. Such a tissue of nonsense and absurdity only owed its fame to the efforts of international Jewry, which had done everything possible to proclaim the deceptive merits of the theory, thus offering irrefutable proof of its limitless power as well as its contempt for truth and reality. Because it was his love of truth and reality that the author of the pamphlet claimed was behind his struggle to preserve what he called German physics from the Jewish corruption infecting it—this same man so blinded by hatred and fear as to have become incapable of perceiving the world in any light other than that of his own obsessions; this same man who was now perfectly satisfied with the reassuring sophism—typical, not of Jews, but of idiots—according to which, since anything that is absurd is incomprehensible, anything we are incapable of understanding must be absurd. It was enough to make you laugh, and also to make you tremble. You did neither. As far as you were concerned, it was quite simply inconceivable that a man of science should demean himself like that and, in so doing, risk demeaning everything he should have been protecting. You were too distraught to laugh and too naive to tremble, you simply couldn't believe that things so manifestly rooted in such complete unreality could have any significant effect other than in the murky depths of a sick mind, and basically, fifteen years later you still couldn't believe it, even though it had become obvious that the movement that had just received its first impulse, or, at least let you glimpse the existence of its long underground course, was having an effect everywhere. Starting in 1933, Jewish scientists, dismissed from universities, deprived of resources overnight without any consideration being given to their value, the blood they had shed for Germany, or simple humanity, had emigrated to England, Ireland, Switzerland, the United States, much to the indifference—the incredible indifference—of their colleagues, who'd mostly refused to sign petitions supporting them, out of conviction, cowardice, or, worse still, mere opportunism, rejoicing that an unexpected stroke of luck had in one fell swoop freed so many posts that their mediocrity had previously forbidden them from aspiring to. Was this the sanctuary of science? Was it this? You envisaged resigning, and, rather than see unreality blight the whole world, as must finally have happened that morning in January 1937, on a street corner in Leipzig, you constantly asked yourself if you shouldn't leave too, as Schrödinger had done, and stop your presence from lending credence to a disgraceful situation, and it's in the little town on the shores of the Mediterranean where I spend the summer of 1995 that echoes of your torment reach me.

We try to understand things on the basis of our own experience because that's all we have, and of course it's quite insufficient, we understand nothing, or we misunderstand, or only understand what's not essential, but what does it matter?

As you know perfectly well, that's the only way we can learn what understanding really means.

In 1995, the world around me doesn't fade away, it doesn't show me its entrails filled with ruins, it doesn't threaten to dissolve from one moment to the next into the nothingness of unreality, but I find it hard to be part of it. In the autumn of the previous year, the army had freed me from the military service I'd constantly put off, getting one deferment after another, convinced that I'd escape it, until the infallibility of the bureaucracy shattered my mad hopes and sent me to rot for ten months in an isolated cavalry camp on a vast damp gray plain, where I divided my time between fatigue duties, useless administrative tasks, reading your books, and a state of paralysis, and now I had no job and nowhere to go. My father asked me to come and stay with him, surrounded by people I know only because I rubbed shoulders with them during the vacations, people whose tireless, ceremonious compassion seemed to have no other purpose than to keep me at a distance. It doesn't upset me, I let them repeat how sorry they are about the woman they no longer call anything other than "your poor mother"—although none of them agreed to meet her when it was still possible. Nothing about my past life is of any concern to me. All I've kept are your books. I've stopped reading them, but I take them everywhere with me; that summer, they get covered with dust next to my bed, in the filthy closet under the stairs that I share with my cousin, to whom my father, tired of the sight of my apathy, has entrusted me for the season so that I can help him in running his restaurant up there on the ramparts overlooking the harbor of an old fortified town that the scourge of tourism has degraded to a seaside resort. Every night, when we close, my cousin hands me an unreasonable amount of money, not without first taking the trouble to call it, with great tact, my "wages," in order to spare me the shame of having to admit to myself that I'm receiving charity, although it's so obvious I'm forced to admit it to myself, without the slightest shame, to be honest—my help consisting of spending my evenings slumped in a large leather club armchair near the cash register, where, drinking everything I can get my hands on, I dream of the novel I will soon write. It will be about a character whose speed and position cannot be determined precisely, who sometimes feels his body spread through the little streets of a town just like this one, covering all the surfaces until other people's eyes force him to materialize at a specific point, and the question of whether he's suffering from an unknown mental disorder or experiencing an unbelievable reality is meant to remain open. But I don't write, I spend my days sleeping and my nights imagining myself following my cousin into all the cabarets and nightclubs in the town, waiting for an endlessly postponed apparition, whereas in truth I'm following in your footsteps, all the way to Berlin in 1933, when you come out after seeing Max Planck, whose wisdom should have freed you from your torment or, at least, assuaged it—that torment so profound that the echoes of it still reach me.

But Planck didn't free you. He had lost hope. Hitler was in the grip of an absurd, morbid hatred that had completely cut him off from reality. Disaster was inevitable and nothing could prevent it, not even sacrifice. For those who, like you, weren't Jewish and didn't support the regime, there were only two alternatives: to emigrate or to remain in Germany. Any university in the world would of course be only too pleased to welcome you, and you would have no difficulty in emigrating. But since you aren't forced to, Planck has suggested you stay in Germany and create what he calls "islands of stability," from which it might be possible, after the disaster, to rebuild what has already started to be destroyed and would by then be even more so. No choice was the right one, he understood that.

To leave would be to allow Philipp Lenard, Johannes Stark, and all the sick minds for whom science bore the traces of its racial origins to take over the universities and impose their own madness on them.

To remain is to condemn oneself to inevitable compromises, like the one to which Planck himself will have to agree a year later, giving the Nazi salute at an inauguration ceremony, making three attempts, as if his old hand, shaking with humiliation, had become as heavy as lead.

You're now walking alone on the streets of Berlin and, even though you will still hesitate for some years, you may have just decided, without even realizing it, that, in spite of the inevitable compromises, in spite of the appeals constantly addressed to you from all sides, in spite of the entreaties that will soon be followed by suspicion, you won't leave, because you want to build one of those "islands of stability"—but how could such islands survive when the movement that's sweeping you along and in which you struggle in vain is so chaotic that the very idea of stability has lost all meaning? How could they survive beneath a surge of such monstrous violence that even an infinitely more radical pessimism than Max Planck's could not have foreseen it? Would Max Planck himself have given the same counsel of resignation if he could have known that on the death of his youngest son, Erwin, hanged in 1945 after the failure of the plot against Hitler, despair would lead him almost to rebel, for the first time in such a long life, against a God he had always faithfully served and who, in return, had protected him from death only to leave him the privilege of burying all his children? It's so easy for me to assert, against the naivety of Planck's pessimism, and the naivety of your own torments, the one superiority I have, the contingent but unquestionable superiority conferred on me by my date of birth. If you'd been able to enjoy that paltry superiority, even for one moment, you might not have made the same decision. But that's by no means certain, since nothing was able to shake it, not even the ever more specific and threatening attacks against you.

You're a traitor, a follower of Bohr and Einstein, an ally of the Jews, a Jew yourself, when it comes down to it, of a kind that's all the more pernicious and malign in that the blood flowing in your veins is unquestionably Aryan, because it's your soul that's thoroughly corrupt, you're "the guardian of the spirit of Einstein," a "white Jew" who Johannes Stark, in the SS newspaper, suggests should be eliminated or sent without further delay to a concentration camp, as an elementary preventive measure, to protect the young from his morbid influence—and those who think they're insulting you in this way confess in spite of themselves that, above and beyond its racial meaning, the word "Jew" simply serves to put together in the same metaphysical category everything that escapes them, everything that makes them sick with fear because they don't understand it.

But you don't leave.

In memory of the time when her husband and your grandfather worked together in a high school in Munich, Himmler's mother agrees to receive yours, and promises that her little Heinrich, who's so kind and affectionate that, in spite of being overburdened with obligations, he never forgets to send her flowers for her birthday, will be sure to make good the injustice done to you—because, she asks, the anxiety in her voice betraying a fear that her question isn't merely rhetorical, there isn't anything leading him astray, is there? Himmler orders an investigation, as a result of which you make regular visits to Gestapo headquarters, trying to retain your self-control as you go in, scrupulously applying the order, pinned up everywhere on the walls, to take a deep breath, haunted by the anxiety that you might suddenly look at the men questioning you with the eyes of a victim, which they won't be able to resist, eyes full of terror, supplication, disgust, defiance, renunciation, eyes that can always be recognized, whatever they express, because they're the eyes of the century. But you're allowed to leave, and you find yourself back out on Prinz-Albrecht-Strasse, relieved and shaking. After a few months, Himmler writes to Heydrich that your death is not desirable. You may be useful. You've earned the right to teach physics as you wish, as long as you don't mention any Jewish names.

Were you so determined to build an "island of stability"? Did the need for that seem so great that you had to end up reproaching Schrödinger for having shirked it by emigrating? Wasn't your stubbornness rather a matter, under it all, of self-esteem, or even of blind, excessive pride? Unless you obeyed that mysterious emotion that I'm incapable of feeling even though I recall seeing it at work. My cousin sometimes seemed to give way beneath an enormous weight that threatened to overwhelm him, and he had to escape, maybe the heat and the constant summer rush, maybe migraine, the memory of sordid nights, or something darker the nature of which I didn't know. He would take me to the mountains to have coffee on the terrace of a lodge in an old herdsmen's village that a hiking trail passes through. We'd stay there for a while, surrounded by cool ferns and tall shady pines, but his mood would remain glum and he wouldn't say a word. We'd get back in his car and go back to town and suddenly, when we least expected it, we'd turn a corner and see the sea. We towered over the landscape, as if suspended in the clear air above the twisting road that plunged through the forest toward the dazzling bay stretching a thousand meters below us. My cousin would open his eyes wide at the sight of this view he'd known since his childhood but seemed to discover each time as if it was the first. He'd make an incredulous grimace, start to smile, and give me little punches on my thigh, saying, fucking hell, man, look at that!—unable to express any more clearly the feeling that was overwhelming him, instantaneously restoring his taste for life, in which it wasn't difficult to see a curious form of love whose object was not another human being, but a quite specific little part of the vast inert world, whose incomparable power I too had to acknowledge, even though I myself was unable to feel it. You of course weren't an uncouth creature like my cousin, you were much more accustomed than he was to confronting the indescribable, but I think you were prey to a similar love, a definitive love, much more powerful than pride, threats, or dreams, a love that, when it came down to it, whatever Planck may have said, left you no alternative. Because of that love, leaving behind you the friends who begged you one last time not to go back to Germany, you'll leave the United States on an almost empty liner and go back to a now inevitable war, but for the moment, you're in your house in Urfeld, maybe in 1938.

You still think there exists another, painful alternative, and your hesitations make you suffer more than ever.

But you lift your eyes to the Walchensee stretching before you, in mist or in bright sunlight, it doesn't matter, and you also greet with an incredulous grimace the power of the love that submerges you, before turning to Elisabeth, squeezing her hands in yours as hard as you can, and saying what it now strikes you you've always known.

My God, how beautiful it is! I'll never be able to leave.

Standing in front of the mirror in his room, Captain Ernst Jünger looks harshly at the Wehrmacht officer facing him, and sees in him nothing but a mocking travesty of his youth. Everything strikes him as being both familiar and curiously misplaced. As quickly as the years pass, they can't be wiped out. They remain, and give the pomp of the uniform he was once so proud to wear an unpleasant tinge of inauthenticity, as if it's been given back to him in the somewhat undignified form of a theatrical costume, tailor-made for a role he's too old to play, and has no desire to play anyway, in a drama he knows well because he was once highly successful in it but whose plot is so unsuited to you that, on you, the same uniform looks like a frankly ridiculous disguise. Rather than think about it, you've tried to consider the training sessions as an opportunity to exercise in the open air. When war is declared, instead of being called up, as you expected, to join a mountain infantry regiment, you are summoned, along with Carl Friedrich von Weizsäcker, to an office in Berlin where it won't take you long to realize that you're soon going to run a greater risk than that of dying in the uniform of a stage soldier.

You're asked to look into the possible practical applications of a discovery that Otto Hahn made the previous year while studying heavy nuclei. By bombarding uranium atoms with neutrons, an obscure change is caused in the material, the appearance of a mysterious element it hasn't yet been possible to identify with any certainty, although some bold conjectures have been advanced, and Otto Hahn has resigned himself to recognizing it as barium, a well-known metal, so ordinary as to be totally devoid of mystery—the only mystery being what it's doing there. The only explanation for that incongruous presence is that a neutron has caused the uranium nucleus to split into two lighter atoms, one of which is of barium, liberating sufficient energy in the process to move a grain of dust. If this fission then gave birth, in sufficient numbers, to neutrons capable of splitting other nuclei, it would start a chain reaction that could be used to produce energy, or an explosive of unsuspected power. The war hasn't yet raised barriers of secrecy everywhere, and thanks to Niels Bohr, who's extremely excited about it, the news spreads from Europe to America. Blackboards around the world are covered with frantic equations, sketched, crossed out, corrected, and endlessly repeated by men who are increasingly febrile, not because they've finally realized, without even wanting to, the dreams of transmutation once dreamed by wizards and alchemists, but because they can already glimpse an exciting and terrible prospect that Niels Bohr still hopes to prove is theoretically impossible: the manufacture of a bomb with such devastating effects that it would be pointless to try to protect oneself from it, just as it's futile to flee death or seek refuge from the wrath of God. But Niels Bohr will have to give up his hopes, because the laws of nature have no use for them. The major theoretical obstacle which should have stood in the way of a bomb shatters and gradually fragments into a series of technical problems, and the Armaments Bureau gives you the task of determining how, and in how short a time, you'll be able to solve them, leaving you free to use, for the success of your mission, as much Jewish physics as necessary.

Did you think, as your friend Carl Friedrich was then convinced, with incredibly childish Machiavellianism, that control of atomic energy would give scientists power over Hitler and allow them to set events on a favorable course? Did you even envisage taking advantage of your situation to preserve German science and keep its youngest and most promising representatives away from the front by claiming that they were indispensable to you? Did you agree to direct the research the better to slow it down and impede it, or simply because, in this place where you'd been carried at an unimaginable speed, you'd long ago left behind you any possibility of refusing? Unless you succumbed, even for a second, although I refuse to believe it, to the toxic enthusiasm of seeing your country regain the greatness of which it had been unfairly deprived, and you wanted to participate with all your heart in its resounding victories, forgetting any concern you might have had about the nature of the masters you were forced to serve.

It's impossible to untangle.

All these stories are perfectly consistent; the most diverse and incompatible of motives would have led you to behave in an absolutely identical way and to take exactly the same decision, and of all these consistent stories in which you appear, in turn, irresponsible, self-sacrificing, upright, complacent, and despicable, nobody can guess which is the true one, especially not me, blindly living through the hot summer of 1995, incapable of perceiving the fear, sadness, and despondency in those around me, even though they're increasingly obvious. Every night, when we get back to our closet under the stairs, where the dirt has reached such an apocalyptic level that the girls who agree to come back with us let out cries of horror when they see it and turn, ready to run—a reaction our diplomatic skills don't always succeed in checking—my cousin asks me to wait on the street until he signals that I can join him, and I obey without even wondering why, while he advances alone toward the dark stairwell, his halting breath still audible a moment longer. Nor do I ask myself why my father seems to be ageing at a prodigious speed between each of his visits, which he devotes, after expressing his ritual anxiety about how terrible I look, to endless discussions with men I've already met but whose faces I won't recognize on the front page of the regional daily paper when they've been gunned down outside the doors, early in the morning, or on the road to some remote village, in their cars, their bloodstained arms hanging outside the car door they haven't had time to open. But I know nothing about blood, apart from the taste of the blood that runs from my nostrils and which I collect on the tip of my tongue, with a stupid smile, in the parking lot of a nightclub where tourists dance and jump in time to the music, raising their arms to the sky. I think less and less about the novel I wanted to write. I devote myself entirely to the childish observation of my decline, which, when it comes down to it, fills me with pride as well as assuaging my creative urges because I imagine it resembles, in its very ignominy, the kind described in Russian novels. I don't see the bloodstained crucifixes in the corners of churches that open their shadowy mouths onto sun-drenched streets. I don't see my father and his friends waging their absurd, invisible war, which doesn't even stop the tourists from jumping on the dance floors in time to the music, their arms raised to the sky, even though it's lasted for a thousand years, without end, without reason, and without glory, with its victims and its killers made indistinguishable through weariness, joined in the same oblivion, the mechanical ceremonies of its bereavements, and it'll never stop because it's never had and will never have any consequence for the future of the world, which weighs on you with all its intolerable weight.

You're working on a nuclear reactor capable of producing energy.

You know it's possible, at the cost of considerable technical effort, to build a bomb that will decide the outcome of the war, and you can't expect your colleagues who've emigrated to the United States not to know that as well as you do.

What a strange movement it is, the movement that's flung you, at a speed no instrument can measure, into the very heart of that which you wanted to escape, and which disgusts you, a place where knowledge is subservient, useful only for the power it promises to provide. You still pretend to believe that it's up to men to decide if this promise must be kept, but you know that power doesn't belong to men, it ignores their dreams of control and walks among them, through them, as indifferent to those who desire it as to those who fear it, holding sovereign sway over all of them. Otto Hahn, after vainly suggesting that all the stocks of uranium should be disposed of, warned that, if the research in which he's participating led to the building of a bomb, he would kill himself, and his resolve, however ridiculous it was, at least bore witness to an unquestionable lucidity, because it concerned only that which can still be decided. For all the rest, it's too late, even though you don't want to admit it and you go all the way to Copenhagen, in September 1941, to have a conversation with Niels Bohr in which you place all your hopes but which will turn out, of course, to be as pointless as it's disastrous. Niels Bohr doesn't listen to you, he doesn't understand what you're getting at, even supposing you understand it yourself, and everything he thinks he understands makes him lose his temper, you're being unforgivably naive, either you're trying cynically to use him in order to pass on false information to the Allies, or you've come looking for an absolution he can't give you because Germany's sins and yours are no concern of his, he isn't and never has been your father, and he isn't even your friend anymore, but you don't realize that, you make a great effort to tell him everything—what you know, what you're doing, what you fear, and what you're planning—in an inextricable jumble of a speech still darkened by the shadow of the bomb, and you draw the diagram of a reactor on a piece of paper, hoping to make it clear to Niels Bohr that it's a reactor you're working on, not a bomb, even though you know now without the slightest doubt that a bomb could be built, but he looks at you in horror, convinced that you've drawn the bomb itself and that you're going to do everything you can to build it.

All these stories are consistent and all are incomplete, as if the principle no longer governed only the relations between position and speed, energy and time, but was now going well beyond the world of atoms, spreading its influence over men, whose thoughts were blurring into the pale hues of indeterminacy.

But that isn't the case.

Thoughts may be hidden, secret, shameful, forgotten, they may be painful, unacceptable, misunderstood, they may be contradictory: they are not indeterminate.

Even though Niels Bohr and you never agreed on what really happened in Copenhagen during that sad autumn night, nor on the words that were uttered, nor on their meaning, nor even on the exact place where they were uttered, something did happen, something that the spells of memory, the wounds, and the feelings of remorse won't be able to change.

Perhaps you're both wrong.

You can't both be right.

It's pointless to look for truth in consistency. But I have the feeling that one day I recognized a familiar smell in a village in Franconia, near the war memorial, on the back of which a timid hand had carved beneath the high grass, almost at the level of the soil, an invisible prayer for the disavowed souls of the defeated—an elusive smell of wet earth, smoke, dreams, and mist, an ageless smell that connects my childhood to yours, and I like to think that this connection, however fragile and tenuous, alone gives me the right to talk to you from the noxious gloom of the closet under the stairs, just as it allows me also to sense a truth I know will always escape me.

You still thought you were the citizen of a spiritual Athens.

In that Athens that no longer existed except in your dreams, you would still have been allowed to go to Copenhagen to entrust what tormented you to Niels

Bohr's inexhaustible kindness, he would have recognized your fear of seeing your work used for military purposes, and your hope that all the physicists in the world would give up the idea of building a bomb because, in that Athens the war hadn't suspended but destroyed, you would still have been Werner Heisenberg, the loyal, brilliant, sensitive Werner Heisenberg, and not the man you'd become in everyone's eyes, the representative of a scorned nation that was occupying Denmark and almost all of Europe and committing despicable crimes, a cursed nation you had refused to leave for illusory or incomprehensible reasons and where, to make things worse, you held official posts, so that your hopes were completely insane, you had no chance of being heard, and even if, by some miracle, Niels Bohr had listened to you, you would have had to suspect that the only conclusion he could possibly draw was that on the pretext of saving the world, you were merely trying to protect Germany from the just punishment that would come to it from the very people it had ignominiously thrown out, and he wouldn't have been entirely wrong, because the image of those you loved buried beneath the ruins of a city flattened by an atomic blast would haunt your nights until the end of the war and, even though you at least understood that your anxieties wouldn't earn you anybody's compassion, you didn't understand much else, you knew perfectly well that your conversation with Niels Bohr hadn't gone well, but you didn't know to what extent hope and fear, and perhaps need, had made you such a poor psychologist that you wrote to Elisabeth, with great delight, that you and Carl Friedrich had spent a last evening with Niels and Margarethe Bohr on the eve of your departure, in a charming setting, and had played them a Mozart sonata, although its joyful A major tonality must have sounded particularly out of place, and you added, again with delight, that you'd walked back to your hotel beneath a wonderful starry sky, that same sky where, two nights earlier, you'd been lucky enough to observe a gorgeous aurora borealis.

But maybe we shouldn't look for truth in the letters that disappointed men send their wives in wartime.

Maybe you're trying, without entirely succeeding, to turn away from the truth as if it were a deadly poison.

The movement that's sweeping you along has taken you so far that those whose respect and trust have illuminated your life now consider you an enemy, nothing will ever be repaired, and it can't be any other way, and to admit it is beyond your strength. Would you have agreed to pay such a price? I don't know, the time to ask the question is long past, nor do I know how fair or unfair your friends are towards you, but I do know that in the spring of 1942, you find yourself in front of Albert Speer, who asks you about the current state of German research into nuclear energy. You talk about your reactor, but Speer turns to you and asks: is an atomic bomb conceivable?

You tell him frankly that it is, at least theoretically, but that its manufacture poses colossal technical problems there's no hope of overcoming—and even then without any guarantee of success—except after several years of unremitting work and a massive investment in manpower and money, so much so that by the end of the meeting, the project isn't given the go-ahead. For your basic research, you demand such a ridiculously modest sum that Speer allocates it to you with an appalled sigh. And while the

Allies, fearing that you might get ahead of them in the race for the bomb, a race in which they think they're competing with you, come up with plans to abduct or kill you, you pursue your attempts to develop a reactor, and you obtain permission for young scientists to be exempted from their military obligations to join you in the relative shelter of your "islands of stability" on which the Royal Air Force never ceases to rain down bombs. You stubbornly carry on living, making children who are born into a world in flames, a world so ugly that nobody can look it in the face without wanting to die, for truth is indeed a deadly poison.

You know that. You saw it destroy Hans Euler, whose thesis you had supervised and for whom you felt such affection. When war was declared, you offered to have him appointed to your laboratory, but he had drunk the poison of truth, and no longer wanted to be saved. He could no longer live among the Nazis, he could no longer live elsewhere, his compatriots' attitude disgusted him, and the rotten souls of men, and he joined the Luftwaffe to carry out reconnaissance flights in the course of which he couldn't kill anybody.

As for himself, he didn't care if he died.

You tried talking to him, the war would end, the world would still be there, a different world, probably not a better world, but it would need men of goodwill to survive in order to at least make sure that it didn't become worse than this one, it was a useful task, a necessary task, some things deserved to be saved from oblivion, but he shook his head sadly, however much you insisted, he no longer believed you, all words of hope seemed to him to give off an unbearable stench, the stench of lies and illusions, and he was suffering terribly, because the effects of the poison of truth are first of all painful, we think nostalgically of the lost sweetness of dreams of the future that we will never have again, the delights of lies and delusions whose stench we can no longer bear after being so long intoxicated by their delicate perfume, the promises of love in which we can no longer believe, but, a few months later, when the poison has dried up even the roots of life, there is no more nostalgia, no more suffering, just the incomparable stillness of despair, and Hans Euler wrote to you from Greece to tell you only about the blue sky, the wine-dark sea, the taste of oranges. His youthful face had grown calmer beneath the curls of his blond hair. He wore an expression similar to that of all young people who, like him, have attained the serenity of a place situated beyond their own death, where they have nothing more to fear and where they live on within the narrow limits of a present that is identical to eternity—First Lieutenant Kurt Wolff and all the dead pilots of Jasta 11, little Ernstel Jünger, the young Soviet tank commander Vasily Grossman met on the Kalmyk steppes, and so many others, they all look life in the face, without regrets and without reproaches, with a childlike gravity full of gentleness. Hans Euler is a hero, maybe the highest kind there is, and you aren't. His death was perfect. As for you, you aren't looking for death, in fact you flee it as much as possible, you don't take any unnecessary risks, and you would never have been so foolhardy as to proclaim publicly, as Ernstel Jünger will do, that if Hitler was hanged, you would walk all the way to Berlin to pull the rope. You're afraid, for those you love and for yourself. You want to live because you know we don't fight a world that devotes all its strength to celebrating an obscene death cult by offering it an extra death, however perfect, but by setting against it the imperfect stubbornness of life, and you're still alive, still stubbornly alive, while Hans Euler's plane goes down in flames over the Sea of Azov and in Italy, near Carrara, a young boy who will never know how *The Charterhouse of Parma* ends lies motionless, his wide-open eyes turned up to the sky, on the marble cliffs his inconsolable father has set up for him like a cradle.

That bastard Schardin doesn't even believe in his own theory anymore!

The Schardin to whom these unkind words of Otto Hahn's are addressed has just given a learned lecture in which he's put forward the delightful idea that the sudden change of pressure during the explosion of a bomb brings about the immediate, painless deaths of those who are lucky enough to find themselves in its proximity, by causing their internal organs to burst, but his brilliant presentation was interrupted by the air-raid sirens and now, not very eager to seize the unexpected opportunity to validate his conjecture, at the cost, admittedly, of the integrity of internal organs that are particularly dear to him, he's huddled in the darkness, surrounded by his terrified listeners, struggling against panic, with Otto Hahn making fun of him, while the blast from the tons of bombs being hurled at Berlin this March night in 1943 shakes the walls of the shelter where you think you've been buried but from which you will all eventually emerge safe and sound. There will be many more underground burial places from which you will have to emerge, to then walk in a city that's already no more than a corpse of a city, through a country that's already no more than a corpse of a country engulfed in the tall red flames of a gigantic funeral pyre, before starting to run at high speed across the pools of phosphorus with, in your heart, a terrible prayer addressed to a God who can no longer be loved but to whom we still turn as if to a cruel and capricious barbarian idol, begging him to let his bombs fall on other people's children, oh, let other people's children die and mine live, and when at last you hug them in your arms, you're ashamed of the selfish, savage joy that takes your breath away, and ashamed of your prayer, but you still have to flee the laboratories and institutes pulverized by bombs, taking with you the heavy water, the rare metals, all the strange things used to feed your experimental atomic reactor, which finally swells, races out of control, and cracks, rumbling like a human heart, before exploding in a jet of molten uranium, leaving you barely time to resume the erratic course that leads you everywhere in Europe, where you give lectures to impassive scientists and watchful spies trying in vain to discover the secret of your soul, while you've already been sent back to the sinister monotony of sirens and invisible bombers roaring in the night over the same corpses of cities made indistinguishable by the ravages of destruction, so that you have the troubling sensation of always being in the same place, as if the endless movement that sweeps you along without a respite, to the point that you fear you will never see the end of it, was nothing, when it came down to it, but an exhausting manifestation of motionlessness.

But there is also another, deeper, more secret movement.

All it can set up against the monotony of chaos is the calm persistence of its imperceptible deployment, which is perhaps enough to prevent the task of deciding what is the truth from being abandoned solely to the worshippers of death.

This movement has no bearing at all on the course of events, it doesn't compensate for any of the horrors, doesn't save a single life, but as long as it persists, the muffled voices of spiritual homelands haven't yet been silenced, hope hasn't been turned once and for all into illusion, nor the truth into poison, and by letting yourself being carried by that movement, every night that you spend writing, you are taken to the sanctuary of a tiny island where no doubt no flower grows, off an isthmus on which, well before you, an old Sufi master was torn between words and silence, a master nobody knows anything about, except for the fact that he too lived in a time of murderers and protected from their rage, so that it could be passed on to the generations, a fragile, precious, living truth, toward which the secret path of metaphor leads. Murderers never discover that path because they don't understand metaphors, they understand nothing but the repulsive bureaucratic code thanks to which they think they can cast the discreet veil of untruth over the grim slaughter they've orchestrated, camouflaging it even from themselves, because the sight of it makes them feel like vomiting. They love death more than anything else, but they can't bear the stench of the corpses with which they exhaust earth and fire, they wish the dead would have the courtesy to fade into nothingness without leaving any trace of their poor lives, and in order to preserve their delicate stomachs from the deadly poison of truth, they have no other choice than to break the link between words and things through lies, until language, deprived of its vital force, stiffens, becomes gangrened, and itself starts to stink like tiresome carrion left in the sun. But in Munich, a few Christian students hope that the stench won't have drowned out the healthy smell of shame to the point that any refusal has become impossible: the refusal to accept an ignominious complicity, the refusal to continue being misled by "a second-rate soldier," author of that "work written in the ugliest German imaginable, which a so-called nation of poets and thinkers has taken for its Bible!" In the name of that minuscule hope, they distribute texts for which they will pay with their lives under the guillotine, without having saved anyone else's, while somewhere in the night, in Leipzig, in Berlin, you echo those thoughts, writing, "That is why those who still know the white rose or can distinguish the sound of the silvery string must now unite." Everywhere in your notebook, you trace escape routes full of life that take you far from the murderers and their dead words and free you from the din, returning you to the task that's always been yours and that of all poets: to go far beyond the resources of language in order to say what can't be said and to describe as precisely as possible all the orders of a hypothetical, multiple, indescribable reality, which sets a mysterious silvery string resounding, although its faint sound never reaches me—and I know now that I will never write my novel, because I'm incapable of telling a story in a language that doesn't exist.

I'm sitting in silence with my father and my cousin on the terrace of the deserted restaurant at two o'clock in the morning. It's the first week of September. A foreign newspaper, bought by my father, lies on the table, and on the front page there's a black-and-white photograph of the body of a man lying right in the middle of a street in one of our towns. Bullet holes can be seen in his chest and his head, which seems to have swelled in a strange way. Here, the local newspaper never publishes photographs of dead bodies, especially not during the tourist season. On the radio, a man's voice, accompanied by an accordion, sings in a language I don't understand. Listening to him, my father can barely hold back his tears, and my cousin can't hold his back at all. A few weeks ago, I don't know why, they shaved their heads, as did all their friends, and the sight of those conspicuously manly faces distorted by emotion strikes me as totally out of place and ridiculous, almost indecent. I look away, and, in order to put an end to the tears and the silence, I ask my cousin what the song says. He wipes his eyes and laboriously translates a few incoherent fragments—*What will we find as an excuse? What will we leave to our children? Why do you kill so many hopes? Our griefs and losses, life here is so hard*—and other fragments too, all having the same clumsy but sincere grandiloquence. But maybe it isn't that grandiloquence that makes them cry. Maybe they're crying simply because, for the first time in years, they're again hearing clumsy but sincere words. My father asks me if I understand what's happening here and, when I lie and answer yes, he says that, in that case, I must also understand that I can't stay, because things have taken such an unpredictable turn he doesn't know if I'm safe anymore. He'll take me to the airport tomorrow, I'll find a life that suits me, somewhere where I'll really be at home, I mustn't worry, he won't let me want for anything, even if something happens to him, and I know that he isn't just sending me away from his pointless, inglorious war to protect me, but because it isn't mine.

I go up to the closet to get my things ready, I wipe the

dust off the covers of your books, which I haven't opened in such a long time, and I find you again, on this night in 1995 when I'm not writing, on that night in 1942 when you write that there is no greater happiness than "the awareness of being at home."

In my language, there's no noun for *home* and we have to resort to clumsy periphrases where your language has that wonderful word that you write in your notebook even though you can't say it, because it's already been irredeemably poisoned and corrupted, like so many other words. In Poznań, addressing a rapt gathering of SS officers, the *Reichsführer* takes great delight in spewing out a thick, nauseating concoction in which every word is given a new, arbitrary, unfailingly odious meaning: cold-blooded murders now bear the name *duty* and we show *tact* if we refrain from referring to them with our accomplices; behaving in a *moral* way doesn't in any way mean, as you write, "being good and helping others," but not taking anything for ourselves, not even a cigarette, from the bodies of those we've just slaughtered; *remaining decent* means standing before their heaped-up corpses and concealing our nausea beneath an appearance of impassivity, or, better still, actually being impassive; *love* refers to the irrepressible urge of the death wish and *the soul* no longer refers to anything at all—a terrible selective sentimentality has taken its place, an almost unlimited faculty for self-pity that doesn't even risk being seen as paradoxical since, in the language of the *Reichsführer*, *executioner* now means *victim*. Somewhere in Byelorussia, an *Einsatzgruppen* rifleman, leaning over a pit, is no doubt moved by his own tact as he stands looking down at the young woman he's taken care to kill first in order to spare her the pain of seeing her child die, while, sitting on their marching kit, some SS officers who've just arrived in Treblinka and haven't yet learned how to remain decent, throw up at the sight of the paths piled high with corpses and complain bitterly of the cruelty of a life that forces them to contemplate such a spectacle; farther south, on the road to the crematoria, *Sonderkommando* prisoners go about their business watched by Rudolf Höss, who also feels sorry for himself for having to put up so valiantly, even though it wounds his sensitive heart, with the painful proximity of these creatures as devoid of compassion as of the most elementary moral sense—and all of them, without exception, whatever their rank and their place in a Europe they have turned into a charnel house, are *victims*, who in addition have to endure the ultimate injustice of remaining forever misunderstood.

But in Paris, Captain Ernst Jünger simply writes in his diary that the Germans have lost the right to complain.

You have to flee the ruins of Berlin and move your institute to Hechingen, south of Stuttgart, where you continue developing your reactor.

In the wake of the Allied armies, Colonel Pash and the men of the Alsos Mission search the abandoned laboratories for information on the progress of the German nuclear program and arrest the scientists who've been taking part in it.

In Strasbourg, in the institute directed by Carl Friedrich von Weizsäcker, the Mission's scientific adviser, Samuel Goudsmit, one of your former Dutch colleagues, long since emigrated to the United States, discovers, no doubt to his immense relief, that you still haven't even managed to develop a reactor.

But he also discovers, with a grief infinitely surpassing his relief, that his hopes of finding his parents, who made the fatal mistake of remaining in the Netherlands and of whom he's had no news since 1943, are in vain. They're long dead, with no other burial than the smoke from a crematorium chimney.

Samuel Goudsmit sleeps in houses abandoned by German dignitaries, surrounded by children's toys and swastika badges.

He smashes the furniture and the dishes, screaming in remorse and hate.

On March 16, 1945, your native city is destroyed by incendiary bombs in less than twenty minutes, and in April Colonel Pash arrives in Hechingen. Your colleagues tell him that you've already left for Urfeld.

The movement that has swept you with it for so long at an indeterminate, almost infinite, almost nonexistent speed will soon come to an end as you cycle every night to rejoin your family in Urfeld, but, as you reach out your hands toward that goal that is so close, space seems to expand and distance the Walchensee, Elisabeth, and your children from you, as quickly as you were hurrying toward them, so that you fear you will never see again, and you advance relentlessly along that road that never ends, listening for the menacing noise of planes searching for targets, you hide in thickets, you're hungry, you pass children scared to death in uniforms that are too big for them, dragging useless rifles, and hordes of unrecognizable ghosts lost in the labyrinth of a defeat so total that your long-ago vision in Leipzig was merely a vague, almost pleasant sketch of it, and yet it seems to you that this defeat is still a victory, perhaps the most complete victory the Nazis have ever won, because they've managed to impose their dream of death to such an extent that it will now engulf them and, with them, the nation that followed them, and their own country that the SS are still crisscrossing tirelessly to make sure, before dying, that nobody escapes death, neither those who persist in their futile resistance nor the defeatists and deserters, all the traitors who've been so incautious as to hang white flags on the fronts of their houses too early because they wanted to live and whose corpses now sway slowly in the wind around the motionless axis of ropes hanging from the branches of trees, beneath the foliage and the frozen buds, where you would have ended up hanged yourself if the SS officer wearily pointing his gun at you hadn't agreed, in return for a pack of cigarettes, to let you continue on your way, in the cold, icy spring that triumphant death has turned to winter, until you manage to reach Urfeld, where you still can't free yourself from the feeling of urgency that oppresses you, as if you were still running at high speed, in spite of the bottle of wine you drink with Elisabeth on the announcement of Hitler's death, while Magda Goebbels, in a gesture of implacable, dazzling logic, poisons her six children, whose corpses in their immaculate nightdresses, their lips turned blue by the cyanide and their hair adorned with the white ribbons their mother tied on them before summoning them all to her funeral feast, are now lined up in front of the soldiers of the Red Army, who take photographs of them, but you, you listen for the shots that still disturb the threatening silence of your sleepless nights until the blessed moment when Colonel Pash opens the door of your house and tells you he has to arrest you and the movement sweeping you along at last ceases and, even though you know you must again leave your wife, and your children cry and reproach you for never keeping your promise to stay with them, you greet the news with a smile full of gratitude and relief, because by now the war is over, you can rest, you can breathe freely and greet the return of the sun, whose rays make the snow on the mountains glitter, the mountains that plunge into the Walchensee, and you so much want to share with someone your joy at again sensing the presence of beauty that you can't stop yourself from turning to the American soldier standing beside you, a stranger who's been walking endlessly in the shadow of death for months, and asking him, as if he's your guest, in a voice throbbing with hope, a question that's strange, thoughtless, or simply innocent, I'm not sure which, a question that for some reason I feel is addressed to me.

Look and tell me, I beg you: what do you think of our lake and our mountains?

ENERGY

In May 1945, Samuel Goudsmit, scientific advisor to the Alsos Mission, travels to Heidelberg to meet with Werner Heisenberg, who answers all his questions with an eagerness that's all the keener in that he doesn't feel as if he's undergoing an interrogation but rather that, after six years of inconvenient interruption, he's resuming a friendly conversation beneath the flowery portals of a spiritual Athens—which, of course, no longer exists. Having magnanimously offered Goudsmit to let his colleagues take advantage of his experience by sharing the results of his research into the development of a nuclear reactor that still doesn't work, he asks him if anyone in the United States has tackled the same question.

Impassively, Samuel Goudsmit says: "No."

Werner Heisenberg believes him.

On July 16, 1945, on the eve of the Potsdam Conference, a dome of fire wreathed in a cloud of transparent purple lights up the sky of New Mexico, leaving a crater of glass and broken emeralds in the desert sand. Robert Oppenheimer, with that tendency toward mysticism more or less shared by all those who've been involved with the atom, evokes, in poetic terms that have become all too celebrated, the intoxicating sense of excess that seizes men when they become gods.

Dragging him away from his meditation on death, time, and the majesty of Vishnu, the man in charge of the Trinity test sums up the situation in a short formula that unfortunately sacrifices mysticism and poetry to a vigorous clarity:

"Now, Robert, we're all sons of bitches."

On August 6, 1945, for no apparent reason, all communication is cut with Hiroshima.

No squadron of bombers has been notified.

A few hours later, a plane sent from Tokyo flies over a heap of smoking ruins stretching as far as the eye can see. In Los Alamos, Robert Oppenheimer raises his arms in a sign of victory in front of a gathering made hysterical by the announcement of their success. Up until the last minute, he was afraid that something wouldn't work. He reminded the military top brass for the hundredth time what the optimum climatic conditions were for all the energy available to be used by the explosion, which must occur at the right altitude, neither too high nor too low, but the bomb has surpassed all the hopes placed in it.

Its rays consumed the flesh of those it touched, it plunged into darkness the awestruck eyes that turned unsuspectingly from a distance toward its magnetic incandescence as if to the friendly light of a star, and it engraved forever on the white skin of the women the dark patterns of their kimonos. The shock wave crossed the city, making bodies vibrate until they broke, tearing apart organs, bringing down buildings that were engulfed in a storm of fire, fanned by the force of unknown winds, while a column of rubble and ashes was sucked up so high into the sky that it soiled the clouds and covered the heads of survivors in heavy drops of black, greasy rain.

The bomb made the acquaintance of its victims, some

of whom, because it offered death new faces, belong only to it. And among them, there are those who, more than others, shared its intimacy and grasped the unaccustomed singularity of its essence. Not of course those who, like so many others before them in so many cities, were buried beneath the ruins of their houses or perished in the fires; nor those who saw their hair fall out or their skin turn to shreds; nor those in whom the part of the body exposed to the radiation was burned to the bone while the rest remained intact and fresh; nor even those killed years later by the radioactive seed secretly planted in them—no: the true casualties of the bomb disappeared without leaving any trace except, perhaps, a vague bright silhouette on a charred wall, frozen in the moment of revelation; the uranium heart beat very close to theirs, they communed with the core of things and returned all at once, without pointless effort, without superfluous stages, to the common substance composing them, which, deep down, like that silhouette, like their memories, like themselves, is nothing.

In a somewhat radical fit of pragmatism, an American general first suggested shooting them. Although presenting the undeniable—and seductive—advantage of simplicity, this solution is not adopted and, on July 3, 1945, after short stays in France and Belgium, the British move ten German scientists who belonged to the various teams working on the Nazi nuclear program into a house called Farm Hall, under the guardianship of Major Rittner, whose orders are to keep their presence secret but to treat them as guests. Their names are as follows:

Professor MAX VON LAUE
Professor OTTO HAHN
Professor WERNER HEISENBERG
Professor WALTHER GERLACH
Dr. PAUL HARTECK
Dr. CARL FRIEDRICH VON WEIZSÄCKER
Dr. KARL WIRTZ
Dr. KURT DIEBNER
Dr. ERICH BAGGE
Dr. HORST KORSCHING

Microphones have been hidden in all the rooms in the house. The guests have all given their word of honor that they won't try to escape or make contact with anyone on the outside.

Among them are world-famous theorists and young researchers. Some have long-lasting, unshakable ties of friendship. Others are barely acquainted, or frankly hate each other. With the notable exception of Professor von Laue, who was a cautious but fierce opponent of the Nazis, the exact nature of their respective relations with the regime remains to be clarified.

Indifferent to such subtleties, British soldiers have categorically refused to serve them, so it's German prisoners of war who take care of their washing and make them the most copious meals they've eaten in six years. Although they're worried about their families, who are still in Germany, and have absolutely no idea how long they will remain in detention, they appreciate the unexpected comfort offered them by the rural setting of Farm Hall. For a time, they almost feel as if they're on vacation.

They take turns organizing lectures on different scientific subjects.

They stroll in the garden.

They play the piano.

They put on weight.

On the evening of August 6, Major Rittner shuts himself upstairs with Professor Hahn, tells him that a uranium bomb has just been dropped on Hiroshima, and sees him snap, as if struck by a single mortal blow. He supports him, puts a glass of gin in his hand, which he has to help him lift to his lips, then pours him another. In an unrecognizable voice, Professor Hahn says over and over that he is guilty, he says that he'd already thought of killing himself when the worst was only a possibility, and now everything has become real. He's surrounded by countless dead. That's a fact. But he's still alive. Major Rittner isn't cruel enough to point that out to him. He contents himself with pouring him more gin and uttering pointless words of comfort, until Professor Hahn feels calm enough to go back down to the living room and announce the news to the other guests.

When the shock wave of Hiroshima reaches them in their turn, it unleashes in them a storm of confused reactions, a mixture of incredulity, horror, relief, curiosity, disappointment, and bitterness. In their stunned amazement, they reveal themselves much more profoundly than they would have wished, or than the demands of modesty or politeness usually allow them. The microphones record the constant, violent, uncertain combat being fought inside them between generosity and selfishness, self-sacrifice and vanity, humility and arrogance, nobility and pettiness.

They're relieved that they didn't build the bomb, they congratulate themselves noisily on the fact, but they're also terribly upset that the Americans succeeded in doing so by shamelessly exploiting a German discovery. The reasons they come up with are contradictory, but they don't care, as long as those reasons provide an honorable explanation for their failure.

They convince themselves that they didn't want to succeed but that, if they'd wanted to, they obviously would have succeeded, unless they would have failed anyway, for lack of raw materials, or because they weren't trusted, or because they would never have been granted the necessary resources in the middle of the war effort, or because Hitler, exasperated at the slowness of their progress, would have cut their heads off, unless, of course, British intelligence had already spared him the bother by taking on the task of eliminating them as soon as the nature of their work was known.

They wander through the house, break up into febrile little groups, find it impossible to get their memories to match up, accuse each other of incompetence or sabotage, or suggest, without much concern for consistency, that they themselves did everything they could to make sure that their research didn't have any military application.

Professor Heisenberg is hurt that Dr. Goudsmit, who he apparently supposes had nothing more urgent to do than to confide a state secret to an enemy physicist, should have had the nerve to tell him such a shameless lie in Heidelberg. He feels ridiculous at having offered to share his knowledge, when it's now clear that nobody in America has anything to learn from him.

All the same, he says he's glad he only worked on a reactor.

Voices are raised, condemning the use of the bomb. Dr. von Weizsäcker is shocked: he asserts that it's "madness."

Professor Heisenberg replies that, on the contrary, it could be considered as having been the quickest way to end the war. But a bit later, he in his turn describes the bombing as "the most diabolical act imaginable." He observes bitterly that, if German scientists had perfected and used such a weapon, they would all have been executed as war criminals.

Professor Hahn hopes that Niels Bohr has not lowered himself so far as to participate in such a monstrous project.

Discovering the recordings, Dr. Goudsmit hears only despicable men trying to rely on their own incompetence in order to draw moral advantage from it, while allowing themselves the luxury, from the height of their own unforgivable compromise, of lecturing those colleagues of theirs who had the courage to fight Nazism. Major Rittner almost chokes at the nerve of these Germans taking offense at the barbarity of Allied military decisions. For a moment he regrets having been so kind to Professor Hahn, who's surrounded by many more dead than he can fear.

Dr. Korsching makes some acerbic and unusually discourteous remarks to Professor Gerlach, who goes up to his room in tears. His despair stubbornly resists all attempts to comfort him. He has no doubt that in Germany he will be held responsible for a defeat he was unable or unwilling to avoid and which has plunged his country into chaos. His compatriots will think that he deserves the ignominious death reserved for traitors, and he's clearly convinced that he himself is one.

As soon as he sets foot on German soil again, someone will kill him.

They'll all be killed, that's for sure.

He continues to shed tears, the meaning of which Professor Hahn doesn't understand. "Are you upset because we didn't make a uranium bomb?" he asks him. "I go down on my knees and thank God we didn't make a uranium bomb. Or are you depressed because the Americans did it before us?"

But no doubt Professor Gerlach no longer understands himself. He can only wander endlessly in the labyrinth of his contradictory feelings of remorse, where nobody wishes to join him.

Later that night, Professor Heisenberg is clearheaded enough to admit that because of the personality of Hitler, the moral problem posed by the development of the bomb couldn't have been the same for German and American scientists.

He makes an effort to comfort Professor Hahn, who's wrong to feel particularly guilty. Supposing that it's even relevant to talk about guilt, that guilt applies to all those, alive or dead, who participated in the development of modern science. A discovery such as nuclear fission only incidentally belongs to an individual. It isn't an end point, it's a stage, more visible than others, more spectacular, perhaps, but no more essential: all stages are essential because they all make up a destiny that amuses itself pretending to be chance.

The bomb might be the destiny of physics, its degradation, its triumph, and its downfall. It's also a fascinating enigma.

"How did they do it?" Professor Heisenberg wonders. "It really would be shameful if we, the professors who worked on it, weren't at least capable of understanding how they did it."

Professor Gerlach's despair seems to have abated. But his curiosity is insatiable. He too now admits: "I really would like to know how they did it."

They still have no idea. Their frustration is immense.

After discussing it for part of the night and coming up with all kinds of conjectures, they've gone back to their rooms, not without first making sure one last time, at the prompting of Professor von Laue, that Professor Hahn won't try to kill himself.

They can't get to sleep.

Until dawn, at regular intervals, the microphones record the cries and plaintive moans of the guests weeping in the dark.

But it's impossible to guess which.

Above all, it's impossible to understand why.

In carrying out his mission, Major Rittner doesn't neglect his gentle but wicked sense of humor.

Dr. Bagge is at the end of his tether. Thoughts of his wife, of whom he's had no news since he left her alone in Hechingen, where French colonial troops undertook to systematically rape all the women as soon as they entered the town, drive him mad with worry. He pours his heart out to Dr. Diebner. He knows that three Moroccans are billeted in his house. He holds back his sobs. In his distress, he compares the conditions of his detention with those in the Nazi camps, even judging them somehow less justifiable in Farm Hall because the war is over.

"They can't do the same thing to us now."

He threatens to start a protest by way of a hunger strike.

Major Rittner has made the following note in the margin of the recording transcripts: *Bagge is much too fat: a diet of bread and water wouldn't do him any harm.*

Among the guests, Dr. Bagge and Dr. Diebner are the only ones who were party members. They fear the British attitude to them, and above all that of their colleagues, their unfair resentment.

They aren't actually guilty of anything.

Dr. Bagge claims to have been enrolled without his knowledge, following an unfortunate initiative of his mother. Dr. Diebner makes it clear that, even though he joined of his own free will, it cost him a great deal of mental anguish, which he would clearly like to be recognized at its true worth. His political beliefs have always been at the opposite extreme from Nazism, and in any case played no role in a choice he made simply in order to gain professional benefits that, in the event of a German victory, would have been reserved for party members, so nobody can reasonably hold it against him. He doesn't doubt for a moment that this is an honorable justification, and one that's enough to absolve him totally.

"I helped so many people!" he sighs.

All of them, without exception, make constant attempts to shrug off their own responsibilities.

They knew nothing of the extent of the slaughter and, although they may only have vaguely suspected it, they all made perilous efforts to oppose it.

They all tried to help colleagues in danger, even though this was often in vain. They make lists of these colleagues and submit them to the other guests, who listen with polite skepticism.

So, for example, Professor Heisenberg was unable to save Jean Cavaillès from the firing squad—Jean Cavaillès who saw no incompatibility between his love of mathematics and political commitment, and for whom the same compelling need governed demonstrative inferences and acts of resistance.

Major Rittner may have become so weary and disgusted at constantly hearing about their pathetic heroism that he ends up totally indifferent to the task of distinguishing truth from falsehood.

In September, he is replaced by Captain Brodie, who writes and signs all the reports.

I don't understand."

Having kindly provided the desired clarification, Professor Heisenberg resumes the little lecture he's giving to the guests on the subject of the uranium bomb, a week after it flattened Hiroshima. This, most likely, is how it works: unlike thermal neutrons, rapid neutrons allow the chain reaction to spread before the rise in temperature has had time to vaporize the load and prevent it from exploding at its full power; the use of a reflector makes it possible to considerably reduce critical mass by sending those neutrons that escape via the surface back to the center of the uranium sphere, where they are able to provoke new fissions; the delicate problem of transportation can be resolved if the fissile matter is divided into two halves that must be hurled toward each other as fast as possible, at the moment of the drop, so that together they reach critical mass.

In exploding, the white-hot uranium sphere would burn two thousand times brighter than the sun. It would radiate so intensely that its unprecedented light might actually come to life, at least for a moment, and sweep away everything, like a strange gust of wind. Then the sphere would dilate, stop burning, and become steam and dust. It would stretch out for a long time across the sky.

It would be over.

The world would no longer be the same.

It is no longer the same.

Maybe Professor Hahn briefly closes his eyes and again feels the presence of the dead around him, their tireless devotion.

"When I was a child," Professor von Laue says, "I wanted to practice physics and see history being made. Well, I've practiced physics and I've seen history made! I'll be able to say that until my dying day." He expresses himself with the bitterness characteristic of those who've seen what it costs to have their wishes granted.

What will practicing physics mean from now on?

The guests imagine that scientists, who alone possess the secrets of the bomb, will have no other choice than to take on major political responsibilities in a new Platonic republic. They envisage this prospect with indifference, eagerness, or disgust.

In the garden of Farm Hall, they already reign over a whole nation of pipe dreams.

Dr. Von Weizsäcker prefers to dream that he will devote himself to philosophy. The others sadly envisage the possibility that they may be prevented from pursuing their work on uranium. They're ready to resign themselves to that. But they're afraid that they may also be forbidden to ever practice physics again. Above all, they're afraid they will never be allowed to go back to Germany for fear they might be tempted to offer their services to the Soviets, unless the Soviets actually abduct them to make sure of their valuable collaboration.

They never doubt their own importance.

They wanted to understand, to look for a moment over God's shoulder.

The beauty of their project seemed to them the greatest that could be imagined.

They'd reached the point where language has its limits, they'd explored a sphere so radically strange that it can only be evoked in metaphors or in the abstraction of mathematical speech, which, basically, is itself nothing but a metaphor.

They constantly had to reinvent what the word *understanding* means.

The knowledge they venerated has been used to perfect a weapon so powerful that it's no longer a weapon, but a symbol of the Apocalypse.

They've all been its oracles and its slaves.

To a remark by Professor Heisenberg suggesting that Dr. Goudsmit of the Alsos Mission might come to their aid, Dr. Wirtz replies: "A man like Goudsmit can't really help us; he lost his parents." And Dr. Harteck adds: "Of course Goudsmit can't forget that we murdered his parents."

But Dr. Harteck, described in the reports as a man of great charm, didn't murder Dr. Goudsmit's parents.

Later, Dr. Wirtz admits to Professor Heisenberg: "We did things that are completely unprecedented. We went to Poland and not only did we murder the Jews of Poland but, for example, the SS showed up at a girls' school, took out the oldest ones, and shot them, simply because the girls were at school and the intelligentsia had to be eliminated. Just imagine if they'd come to Hechingen, showed up at a school, and shot all the girls! That's what we did."

But Wirtz, described in the reports as intelligent, sly, and self-centered, didn't shoot those schoolgirls.

Obviously, none of the guests killed anybody. They probably never even dreamed of it, except perhaps in those obscure fantasies on which dreams and anger sometimes cast a fleeting light. But they know what they must answer for collectively. Their differences, dislikes, and rivalries cannot keep them apart forever. When they have to talk about the killings, a single personal pronoun rises reluctantly to their lips—*we*. This *we* keeps them all united within its ring of steel. They didn't kill anybody, that's the truth, but they know that, in a way, each of them closed the gas chamber door on Dr. Goudsmit's parents. Each of them raised a steady hand and shot a Polish schoolgirl.

Perhaps they remember the words of the students of the White Rose, whose echo they hear: "Everyone is guilty, guilty, guilty!"

They say: "Our lakes and our mountains."

They say: "This is what we've done."

But that doesn't mean: "These are our lakes and mountains. This is our crime."

On the contrary, it must be understood as: "Since we're part of the lakes and mountains, we're also part of the crime."

All the same, they talk about the risks they took, bravely and alone.

They try to again become individuals in order to break the spell of their collective utterance.

Perhaps they still hear: "The end will be terrible."

There's something sad and ridiculous about their efforts.

They have demands.

They're convinced that something is owed to them.

They assume that the Allies have nothing more important to do than to crisscross Germany delivering their letters and bringing their loved ones' replies back to England.

They imagine that their torments matter.

They live in a world that doesn't exist.

When the mail is late, they become anxious, hostile, vulnerable. They weep.

Professor von Laue triumphantly brandishes the letter he's just received from his son. He wants to share his joy. Those who've received nothing throw him nasty smiles and sidelong glances, overflowing with a dark jealousy that resembles hatred.

Dr. Bagge learns at last that his wife hasn't been raped. He's briefly euphoric. But then he quickly finds a new reason to be morose, complaining bitterly that she's been forced to cook for the French.

Dr. Diebner's problems are quite different. With infinite tact, Captain Brodie tells him that it hasn't been possible to get his letters to his wife, because she's run off with another man and hasn't left a forwarding address. Dr. Diebner seems to adapt with remarkable stoicism to his new situation as a cuckolded husband. He says he's glad that someone is looking after his wife. Maybe he hasn't quite grasped the exact nature of the news.

As the principle stipulates, in a very short space of time, the indeterminacy of energy is such that it can go through considerable variations in intensity, and can even emerge abruptly out of nothingness; but if the time drags on, as it does in Farm Hall, without ascribable limits, it invariably regains the monotony of its basic level, its lowest level.

They're all bored to death.

Something in them becomes gradually worn-out over the endless weeks.

Professor Heisenberg plays Mozart sonatas, by heart, on the piano. Nobody listens to him anymore. Every day, Professor Hahn walks for hours in the garden, never tiring. He calculates the distance he's covered. If he'd walked straight ahead, he would have crossed the sea. By now, he would have been in Germany for ages.

The guests are sometimes visited by British physicists. Patrick Blackett. Sir Charles Darwin. Sir Charles Frank. They discuss theoretical problems with new ardor, the nuclear reactor, heavy water, the separation of the isotopes. They talk about their dreams of the future, their return to Germany, the laboratories, the universities, everything that will need to be rebuilt. Beyond the garden of Farm Hall, a wider world still exists of whose intoxicating presence they again become aware. Professor Gerlach is in a mischievous mood: "What Sir Charles says isn't completely stupid!" They all burst out laughing. The memory of Wolfgang Pauli's unbelievable nerve takes them back for a moment to the paradise of the 1920s. But of course Sir Charles leaves in the end, and every visit acts as a bomb blast whose shock waves, increased by boredom, spread for a long time through the emptiness of Farm Hall, provoking sudden patches of turbulence.

The guests grow agitated, they overflow with useless energy, which they expend on futile discussions.

They're suddenly convinced that the whole of the international scientific community is concerned about their fate.

They write endless letters, they squabble.

They make futile plans, lose themselves in absurd schemes, because they no longer have any doubt that their demeanor and their decisions are capable of bringing about a change in their situation.

They endlessly calculate the probability of seeing their families and country again. Their estimates reflect with mathematical precision the constant fluctuations in their fickle moods, confidence and depression, euphoria and despair and impatience, the motionless hours painfully illumined by the vague memory of a loving or unfaithful wife. They're afraid of one day forgetting their children's faces.

Professor Heisenberg has perfected a little turn that he reiterates endlessly. Whenever the guests have gone too long without news of their families, or whenever they suddenly decide that they need immediate answers to all the questions they're asking themselves about their future or the length of their detention, Professor Heisenberg marches into Captain Brodie's office with a serious threat: if their just demands aren't taken into account by the authorities, he'll break his word and immediately announce his presence in Cambridge. After this same scene has been repeated with tiny variations at increasingly short intervals, Captain Brodie finds it hard to stop himself from laughing in Heisenberg's face. But he never does so. Because he has to make sure of the guests' cooperation and can't run the risk of offending them. And because he likes Professor Heisenberg a lot. Apart from anything else, he's an ideal prisoner. In the vast slaughterhouse that Europe has become, he still feels so bound by his word of honor as to make chains, bars, and jailers seem perfectly pointless. He holds such store by it that he doesn't doubt the effectiveness of his terrible threat, even though of course it has absolutely no effect.

They're remarkably intelligent men all the same.
They've entered the sanctuary of the master of Delphi.
They understand what to most men remains a mystery.

But they don't understand that they're no longer masters of their own fates. They don't understand that nobody cares what they want, or that their constant demands are pointless and annoying. They don't understand what being defeated means because, when it comes down to it, they don't even understand that they've lost the war.

No, the simplest things they don't understand.

In November, the *Daily Telegraph* announces that the Swedish Royal Academy of Sciences has decided to award the 1944 Nobel Prize for chemistry to Professor Hahn, in recognition of his discovery of nuclear fission. The guests organize a celebration meal, to which they invite Captain Brodie. At the tops of their lungs, they sing the words of a rough, humorous poem in an unlikely mixture of English and German, jokingly accusing Professor Hahn of being responsible for all the ills of the world, and when they come to the chorus they bang on the table and cry in unison: "And who's to blame? Otto Hahn!"

They're as merry, carefree, and unruly as a band of old students.

Professor Hahn proclaims that, if he's granted permission to go to Stockholm, he fully intends to get totally plastered with his Swedish friends, as the honor paid him demands.

Everything, though, is spoiled when Professor von Laue is tactlessly unable to stop himself from including Frau Edith Hahn in his fulsome tribute to her husband, thus unwittingly summoning the cherished shades of absent wives to the banquet table, where they silently take their places, bringing with them their forgotten perfumes and the distant gentleness of lost homes. Professor Hahn passes instantaneously from joy to tears. Not to be outdone, Professor von Laue now also bursts into sobs. Stuck between the two distraught men, Captain Brodie makes an effort to keep up a dignified front in order to conceal the awful embarrassment into which this painful scene has plunged him. Above all, he's afraid the contagion might spread to the other guests, who, not wishing to pass up this unique opportunity to feel sorry for themselves in their shared misery, would collectively inflict on him the distressing, tearstained spectacle of their sorrow.

In the days that follow, Professor Hahn waits in vain for official confirmation of his Nobel Prize. He suspects Captain Brodie of taking a wicked pleasure in keeping him on tenterhooks. He demands to be allowed to write to Stockholm, to avoid the Royal Academy being offended at his incomprehensible silence. He feels forever dishonored. He loses his temper and screams that he can no longer answer for anything. He wishes the worst disasters to befall the United Kingdom. Professor Heisenberg is unable to calm him down.

Just before Christmas, the guests learn that, having been detained for six months, as permitted by British law, without any other reason than His Majesty's pleasure, they will all go back to Germany at the beginning of January 1946.

They forget their sadness, their resentments, the certainty they sometimes had that they were being subjected gratuitously, out of pure sadism, to pointless mental torture.

They speak of their stay at Farm Hall as if it were a delightful vacation.

Dr. von Weizsäcker claims with suspect enthusiasm that he would gladly spend another six months there.

They think it would be more prudent for them not to tell anyone in Germany how they've been treated.

They fear they would be accused of collaboration.

But they want nevertheless to express their gratitude. For Christmas, they give Captain Brodie a souvenir album they've put together for the occasion. Each of them has written his own biography, leaving a blank space above the text for his photograph. They have no photographs. They promise they will provide them later. They won't have the opportunity to do so. And Captain Brodie's Christmas gift will end up in the records of British intelligence.

On the flyleaf, in pencil, pen, or charcoal, someone has drawn Farm Hall.

Professor Hahn has written:

At the beginning of 1944, my institute in Dahlem was entirely destroyed by bombs. I transferred my activities to Tailfingen, in Württemberg, where I was arrested by American soldiers on April 25, 1945.

Dr. von Weizsäcker has written:

Even more than science in the abstract, it is its significance for the spirit of the time and its relationship with philosophy and religion that arouse my interest.

Professor Heisenberg has written:

I, Werner Karl Heisenberg, was born on December 5,

1901, in Würzburg, where my father taught high school and was an assistant at the University. In 1909, my father was transferred to Munich; it was there that I grew up, learning languages, mathematics, and music. From 1920—after a short interval as a volunteer soldier—I studied physics there with Sommerfeld. At the same time, I joined the youth movement, regularly participated in cross-country hikes, and practiced all kinds of sport. In 1924, I became an assistant at Göttingen and invented quantum mechanics during a stay on Heligoland. In 1926 and 1927, I was an assistant in Copenhagen, and a pupil and friend of the great physicist and philosopher Niels Bohr. From 1927 to 1941, I was a professor at the University of Leipzig, where I taught atomic physics to a large number of students, both German and foreign. In 1929, I gave classes and lectures in America, Japan, and India. I have had a family since 1937. In 1941, during the war, I was transferred to the Kaiser Wilhelm Institute of Physics.

And no doubt there is nothing more to be said.

On January 3, 1946, accompanied by Major Rittner and Captain Brodie, they land in Germany, in a landscape of ruins and rubble. They will have to live surrounded by it for years to come, but for the moment they pretend not to see it.

They travel through the occupation zones to Hamburg, Göttingen, Bonn, and Munich, watched by Allied soldiers and Soviet spies.

They look for places to settle.

They request authorizations that are sometimes only granted after an endless wait.

They hope that something will finally emerge from the ruins.

In spite of his tactlessness at Farm Hall, it is to Max von Laue that the honor falls to give, before a gathering of physicists, the eulogy for Max Planck, whose pupil he was and who, after gradually losing everything in the course of far too long a life—his house, his library, his manuscripts, and all his children—has at last found an island of stability where he may forget to ask God for an explanation.

While in Washington, in a melodramatic gesture of despair, Robert Oppenheimer holds his long, pale hands out in front of him, arms open and fingers trembling, so that President Truman can certify that they're covered in blood, Werner Heisenberg flies to Copenhagen, where he will complete his apprenticeship in the need for silence. Because he'll never be able, as he still hopes he will, to justify himself to Niels Bohr and will have to concede that, for their relationship to continue, it would be best never again to mention their encounter in 1941, or anything relating to the war. So they talk of other things. Pi mesons. The aurora borealis. The future.

But they can't forget that, in spite of his regrettable fondness for sententious turns of phrase, Oppenheimer is absolutely right: physicists have known sin, a sin that is much too big for them.

They have all fallen, all of them, all at once.

And Werner Heisenberg, whose dazzling youth has abruptly vanished without a trace, may be thinking that a long time ago, at the end of another war, in a time of defeat and revolutions, an old mathematician and his devil dog had a mysterious presentiment of it. Professor von Lindemann had seen what the shy boy who wanted to study mathematics and was then standing full of hope in front of his desk already bore within him without even knowing it.

An evil energy, silently radiating.

The seeds of sin, its indelible stain.

The promise of a destiny pretending to be chance, the inevitable achievement of which would be at one and the same time a triumph, a fall, and a curse.

Professor von Lindemann couldn't help but be seized with a holy terror and chase away that boy in whom Werner Heisenberg may not recognize himself but who nevertheless arouses in him an irresistible nostalgia, not for youth, but for lost innocence.

TIME

From the sultanate of Oman to the shores of the Gulf, of which the Persians and the Arabs still contest the honor of being the eponymous heroes, across the sands that were the age-old home of Bedouin for whom no beauty, except that of God, was greater than the beauty of poetry, there may still be men dazzled by the incomparable lines that Al-Mutanabbi composed more than a thousand years ago:

The horse, the night, and the desert all know me,
And so do the bow, the sword, the paper and the pen.

But nobody these days can ascribe the boundless pride of those lines to themselves. They've become the silent relics of a world that's vanished abruptly, an ancient treasure, strange and venerated, which glitters now with an incomprehensible glow in the shrine of an empty temple. In less than forty years, on the sand of the desert, on the shore of the burning sea where poor pearl fishers once dived all summer long, oil has fertilized the arid earth and brought forth towers of glass, marble, and steel that thrust ever higher into the dusty furnaces of the sky. Hidden behind the tinted glass panes of their luxury cars, the children of the Bedouin, whose lofty destitution was so admired by occasional British adventurers, and who today have lost even the memory of their former poverty, casually ride through vast cities where tourists and businessmen, financiers, princes, slaves, and whores rub shoulders. The ancient silence throbs with the incessant hum of air conditioners, and echoes day and night with all the languages in the world. In the evening, the pale disk of the sun slowly descends onto a horizon bristling with cranes and billboards.

The hotels, the businesses, the restaurants, the boutiques lined up in the colossal aisles of the shopping malls, everything that emerges from the earth, must be given a name.

Everything must be transfigured by lies.

We are not the master of Delphi, who neither speaks nor hides his meaning. Our words are simply human. They can only reveal the world imperfectly or bury it in lies—and thus attain perfection. I'm very well acquainted with the art of giving deceptive names to things, the art of shopkeepers and politicians. At the end of a road that, however unlikely, I know owes nothing to chance, I've finally learned many things. I've learned to arouse that vain, compulsive appetite that's become the only face of desire. I've learned to make everything that's base glitter. I've learned to turn all ideas into sales pitches. That's the only way the study of letters and philosophy can still justify their existence in this world, by producing men like me who've finally understood how to make their *creativity* effective.

I can say anything.

I can even allow myself to mention death.

I call it *eternity* or *heritage*. I call it *serenity*. Those who hear me are no longer afraid. They smile and think of the passage of time—death, the destroyer of worlds—as if it were a friend. They buy luxury products that are supposed to survive them and may indeed survive them after all.

You see, there really is nothing to be done: when it comes down to it, all I've been able to do is move ever further away from you, just as, admittedly, you never ceased moving so painfully away from yourself. At least I've never had to live up to a poet's vocation in a world where, like the verses of Al-Mutanabbi, it no longer means anything.

You asked: "What is strong?"

You spoke of the white rose and the mysterious sound of the silvery string.

You wrote that the scientist must also be a priest and that there's a place where we can be sure that the love of God doesn't lie.

Do you remember entering a vast hall in the Technical University of Munich in November 1953, having been invited by the Bavarian Academy of Fine Arts? A year earlier, an island in the archipelago of Eniwetok vanished into thin air after the explosion of the first American thermonuclear bomb. All that remains of it is an underwater crater. And invisible radiation. And the unknown heavy metals forged by the bomb, slumbering in the waters of the Pacific. You must miss the days when people could still afford the luxury of surprise and alarm. It's all become so sadly predictable. After a time, the worst curses become monotonous.

In the photograph the English took in the garden of Farm Hall in 1945, you had already aged so terribly, as if for you the war had lasted a hundred years. But today, as you stand in that hall at the University in Munich, a few minutes before giving your lecture on "The image of nature in contemporary physics," and lean toward Ernst Jünger as if to whisper something confidential, while, sitting a few rows in front of you, Martin Heidegger smiles in a self-satisfied way, I even hesitate to recognize you. You're fifty-one years old and, next to you, Ernst Jünger almost looks like a young man. How is it possible? Somehow you'd remained yourself for so long, so stubbornly young. Your youth has vanished and I know that it vanished in one fell swoop. The new physics you helped to found, when you still looked like a carefree boy scout, has burst all continuous lines into a broken series of discrete events separated by dark chasms. Maybe the line of time hasn't been spared. One morning, we look in the mirror and see the astonished face of a stranger. We leave somewhere in Wilson's chamber a new drop of condensation briefly illuminating the fog. We trace a pretense of a trajectory, but we know perfectly well that we carry with us the memories of another.

Remember, there is no trajectory: it's from you that I learned that.

There's probably no continuity either.

As you and Ernst Jünger exchange a few words, an incredibly youthful smile suddenly lights up your deeply-lined face. The vague shadow of those lines could already be glimpsed on your childhood photographs, and the alert young professor from Leipzig who couldn't be differentiated from his students must sometimes have shuddered and stooped inexplicably on sensing the silent presence of the old man he had always carried inside him. Do you remember what Einstein thought, when he indulged in metaphysical speculations? Everything is given once and for all, the vast universe and each of our lives, our tiny love affairs, as one compact block of inaccessible eternity, which our minds run through and roll out for us as a continuous flow, like the tip of a diamond following the grooves of an endless record. If that's the case, then in a way something still remains of your vanished youth as you leave Ernst Jünger and cross the packed hall in the Technical University of Munich. I imagine Martin Heidegger, who the next day will give his lecture on "The question of technique" to an even more incredible number of people, watching with subtle condescension as you make your way to the rostrum. The audience fills every space on the benches. The Munich students refuse to politely give up their places to the visitors who've come from all over West Germany. Nobody respects the safety instructions. You move forward laboriously in such an atmosphere of intellectual fervor that you might almost think yourself back in a reborn Athens, although you know it isn't so.

You once asked: "What is strong?"

You answered that it was the almost inaudible sound of a silvery string.

Today, you say:

"Technique is almost no longer seen as the result of conscious human efforts to increase material power, but rather as a large-scale biological event in the course of which the internal structures of the human organism are increasingly transported into the surrounding world; it is thus a biological process which by its very nature is outside the control of man; for 'even if man can do what he wants, he cannot want what he wants.'"

I haven't abandoned you, you see: your words still reach me as I sit here, for the last time, in a taxi driving to the airport along Sheikh Zayed Road, one evening in September 2009. Beneath the orange lighting of a parking lot, Indians dressed in awful sweat-soaked checkered shirts argue as they play cricket. The tallest tower in the world rises in the darkness like the spire of a huge cathedral—no, you're right, it rises rather like a monstrous carnivorous plant, sinking its roots deep into the sand of the desert, and it's the whole city that's a giant organism, pulsing with the force of a new, pitiless, primitive life, which in every way resembles the life that pulses in us too, with its abrupt spurts in growth, its erratic greed, its insane prodigality, its infections, its cancers, and its rottenness. Nothing is lacking here, not even blood : the whole city is bound together by the blood it has fed upon, and still feeds upon. Indian blood, Pakistani blood, the blood of Bangladesh, Nepal, and Sri Lanka, all that anonymous blood that flows tirelessly in its steel veins and makes it proliferate, indifferent to the approval or disapproval of men, whom it returns to their impotent solitude. They built it, but it owes them nothing. And the death that threatens it today won't come from them.

The towers of the Marina that are still under construction offer their naked entrails to the scorching sun. The cranes have been motionless for weeks. The workers squat in silence, waiting for their wretched wages that won't come, while, beyond the shores of the Gulf, mothers who've forgotten their faces shower curses on them. The disease has spread, from one financial center to another, through intangible networks, into the great body of the world, and has even reached here. A slow paralysis is creeping over all the vital organs of the city, which pants like a dying animal. No sooner is it born that it's about to die. Nowhere else, ever, has the blind process of life and death manifested its uncontrollable power with such purity, never has it taken place with such terrifying speed. You probably wouldn't be surprised. You know that in a very short space of time, an almost infinite energy can emerge from nothingness then go back to it.

You wrote that there's a place where the love of God doesn't lie.

But, as you say today to the silent crowd listening to you in Munich, instead of that love man no longer meets anything but himself. Strange excrescences of our organs have inexorably overrun the world. They've transformed it. Flesh has become glass and metal. Long nerves of copper snake through the darkness of the shafts drilled in the concrete. Incinerators digest the tons of garbage dumped day and night by endless lines of trucks crossing the desert. The workers, exhausted by dehydration, are eliminated like toxins. The cold eyes of the security cameras never close. Blood remains blood.

On the road to the airport, the taxi driver, who's very young, suddenly turns and tells me in a beseeching voice that he's constantly afraid in this vast city.

He's just come from Nepal.

He misses his family.

He didn't know it was possible to be so alone.

I put my headphones on and listen to Depeche Mode, at high volume, as if I were twenty, watching the skyscrapers parade past. The driver stops speaking. Nothing can save from solitude a man who's stopped meeting anyone but himself. That's the way it is. This world that extends and reflects us is more terrifying, more alien, more hostile than wild nature ever was, and I can do nothing about it.

You wrote that the scientist must also become a priest.

But you've known for a long time that his sin makes that impossible. It isn't up to him to choose what he must become—an engineer, a technician, a hired hand responding servilely to the sovereign injunctions of an inhuman voice, as we all zealously respond to it, concealing our weakness beneath the vulgar mask of arrogance. Our creativity, our rebellions, our noisy displays of irreverence are nothing more than the pitiful symptoms of an unprecedented submission. The island of Heligoland is a long way away, its dazzling beauty. The castle of the prince of Denmark. The flower-filled springtime of Göttingen. Youth and faith. You've lost so much. You tell Elisabeth how glad you are that you've sometimes been able to glance over God's shoulder. You'll once again sit beside Niels Bohr at the foot of the Acropolis. You'll exchange letters with Wolfgang Pauli. But what the war has broken will not be mended. And your disagreements with Einstein are no longer of any interest to anyone. They've never had the slightest practical application, which these days means that they're quite simply worthless. You can't helping thinking sadly of them as you evoke to your listeners in Munich the possibility of escaping the danger of the biological process you've just described, a danger all the greater since it takes on the exhilarating appearance of progress, a danger I know, from the height of the superiority conferred on me by my date of birth, that we will never escape, Heidegger may well quote Hölderlin with mysterious grandiloquence, applauded to the rafters by delighted students, but we shan't escape it. That process will continue all the way to its inconceivable end, it will subject everything to the tyranny of its growth with such radical intransigence that nothing will be spared, not even the sanctuary to which you were refused entry by Professor von Lindemann's little dog leaping so vehemently one day in 1920, because you threatened its purity and, if he could have witnessed it, old von Lindemann himself would have had to admit, much to his despair, that mathematicians too had known sin—if only he could have seen them in their City offices, developing the infallible algorithms that determine, at a speed the human mind can't even imagine, decisions to buy and sell in all the markets of the world.

But the markets have collapsed, in one financial center after another, even here on the shores of the Gulf. The designers of algorithms are shaking in impotent dread. Soon perhaps, the skyscrapers strung out along Sheikh Zayed Road, and the tallest tower in the world itself, will be abandoned to the sands of the desert and the wind will carry the acrid smell of their metallic rottenness all the way to Iran. Their decay will be much slower than their birth. They will stand for a long time by the sea, their mummy-like bones eroded by salt. They may become an object of fearful fascination to men who will be unable to figure out the secret of their fleeting existence. Nothing more will emerge from the ground, waiting to be named.

In a few months, my activities have been reduced to almost nothing. The telephone has stopped ringing. I check my e-mails out of habit. Soon I won't be able to pay my employees or pay back my loans. Soon, the art of lying will have become useless. Here, there's no other remedy for bankruptcy than prison. The rich are the first to flee, as I myself am fleeing. Then it'll be the turn of the Filipino housemaids, the Russian and Nigerian whores. The workers will go somewhere else to die, of hunger, thirst, despair, everything the poor die of. I may miss the plate-glass windows of my living room looking down on Jumeirah Beach, the tall figures of the abaya-clad young women I've never been able to talk to, the red leather seats of my sedan, the wonderful glitter of its bodywork caressed every week, with infinite gentleness, by the chamois leathers of the sweat-drenched Pakistani cleaners in the underground parking garages of the shopping malls. At the airport, I give the taxi driver all the cash I have left and won't be able to use anymore.

He takes my hand effusively.

He's on the verge of tears.

He's very young, maybe nineteen.

He murmurs words of insult or blessing in his language.

His gratitude is more unbearable to me than his hatred.

In the end, it's quite likely I won't miss any of it. I'm taking nothing with me but one item of hand baggage. I'm supposed to be taking a short business trip. But it's not just a question of caution. What's the point of being loaded down with pointless remnants? We can't only half change our lives. In my apartment, the closets are full of clothes I've abandoned to mildew without any regrets because they're no longer mine. In the first-class lounge, the receptionist smiles at me. I see it as a tribute to the end of this life, a brief, solitary twinkle in the cloud chamber. This life too will grow blurred, it'll join the ghosts of other lives, lost in limbo, between the possible and the real, to which nothing connects it. I may have been a childish, conceited student, and a young man lost in the twists and turns of an absurd war he didn't understand, but they're nothing to me, I feel no closer to them than I do to the British captain who received you patiently in his office in Farm Hall and laughed at your naivety; and very soon, for sure, I'll think of that foreigner drinking a glass of champagne in the first-class lounge with a smile on his face the way we think of a dream.

You asked: "What is strong?"

You replied that it was the white rose, the almost inaudible sound of the silvery string, and, I remember, it was then that I realized what you meant. I thought you were right and, in a sense, you know, I still think that. Because, like you, I may have been many things I don't recognize and to which I owe nothing, and now at last I'm free to join you, across the broken lines of time, as I've so much longed to do. I don't want to disturb your happiness, looking out at the North Sea from the island of Heligoland, I don't want to butt into your exhausting discussions with Niels Bohr, nor do I want your orphaned eyes to turn away, just because of me, from the cloud chamber where the principle awaits you, no, I prefer to stand beside you in Urfeld, in May 1945, by the Walchensee, when the din of the war has fallen silent and it's again possible to hear the crystalline, almost imperceptible sound of the silvery string.

You've just cycled across what remains of Germany to rejoin your family. You've passed SS officers, children, frozen trees, and hanged men.

I'm an American soldier from the Alsos Mission.

I don't even know my own name. All I know is that for a long time I've been advancing in the shadow of death, across a ruined continent that's stopped being the center of the world. I've seen corpses walking. I still have in my nostrils the smell of decay, the smell of flesh, the smell of the engines of ripped-open tanks lying in viscous pools of oil and blood. And now I'm standing beside you, facing an unknown lake surrounded by snowcapped mountains beneath a blue sky lit by an icy sun.

To me, you're merely an enemy scientist whose work is of great interest to our intelligence services, though I probably have no idea why.

You're sitting beside me, smiling wearily.

I find it hard to believe you're only forty-three.

I don't know what's made you age like that.

Very likely, I don't care.

You then turn to me and ask, with incredible cordiality, an extraordinary question:

What do you think of our lakes and our mountains?

I should feel surprise, or cold anger. I should answer curtly that you have no right to ask a question like that, not you, not now, or I should turn my back on you with contempt, abandon you to your thoughtlessness. I should suppress a violent gesture. But I lean toward you and see your face glow with such disarming trust that I find it hard to lose my temper.

You smile at me with a smile of eternal youth.

I look at your lake and your mountains, I look at you

again, I may hear a sound so long covered by the screams, the weeping, and the whizzing of bombs, a soft, distant sound, the notes of an immortal chaconne rising from a solo violin that's never fallen silent. And I realize that the question you ask me is neither out of place nor pointless. How could I be your enemy?

You ask again, insistently:

Look and tell me, I beg you: have you ever seen anything more beautiful?

And because I've at last joined you in this place where it's impossible for God's love to lie, I place a hand on your shoulder, smile back at you, and reply:

No.

Oh, no, I assure you.

I've never seen anything more beautiful in my life.

AUTHOR'S NOTE

I have mainly drawn the historical material of this novel from Werner Heisenberg's autobiography, *Der Teil und das Ganze*, and the memoirs of Elisabeth Heisenberg. I have also made use of Thomas Powers's extremely well documented book, *Heisenberg's War*.

The third part, "energy," is based on the recordings made at Farm Hall between July and December 1945, which were made public in 1993.

I have received valuable support in Germany.

I should like to thank Christian Ruzicska for his constant help and Martin Heisenberg, who agreed to speak to me about his father.

My debt to Cornelia Ruhe, professor of Romance Literature at the University of Mannheim, is immeasurable. With tireless generosity, she translated Werner Heisenberg's correspondence for me. May she receive this novel as a sign of gratitude and, even more, of friendship to her, as well as to Bernd, Oscar, and Mathilda, from this side of the Rhine.

About the Author

Jérôme Ferrari is a writer and translator born in 1968 in Paris. His 2012 novel, *The Sermon on the Fall of Rome*, won the Goncourt Prize. He is also the author of *Where I Left My Soul* (MacLehose, 2012).